Mississippi Mojo
...and Murder

Tale of the Blues

Mary S. Palmer

&

Paula Lenor Webb

Mary S. Palmer & Paula Lenor Webb

An Intellect Publishing Book
Copyright 2021 Mary S. Palmer & Paula Lenor Webb

ISBN: 978-1-954693-33-3

Front cover design by Abe Partridge
Songs by Mike Turner and Mary S. Palmer

First Edition: 2021

VFV-4PB

Visit the website: www.MississippiMurderBook.com

Intellect Publishing, LLC
6581 County Road 32, Suite 1744
Point Clear, AL 36564
www.IntellectPublishing.com

Acknowledgments

Many thanks to our wonderful Beta readers, Shannon Brown, Mary Duffy, Muriel Nero, Mike Turner, and David Preston. Without their input, this book wouldn't be the same.

We appreciate their thoughtful critiques.

Mary S. Palmer & Paula Lenor Webb

Dedication

To my mother, Janie Cashin Schluter, who always encouraged me in any of my endeavors

Mary S. Palmer

To those wonderful people I met when I lived in the Mississippi Delta

Paula Lenor Webb

Mary S. Palmer & Paula Lenor Webb

Prologue

The splatter of rain on the tin roof awakened Mama Cheche Brown. The rhythmic beat of the drops intensified, becoming large streams. She tilted her head, listening as they blended together in the grooves of rusted metal sheeting on top of her row house. The sound morphed into a trickle as water rolled off the eaves and landed in the dark Delta farmland surrounding her home. The rainwater splashing on the tin reverberated to her body, running a chill up her spine.

Mama Cheche's shoulders shook. "Lordy, me. Can I make it through one more summer? This weather's gonna be the death of me yet." The box springs on her iron bed squeaked when she got up. Ignoring the familiar noise, she slipped on her dressing gown, walked to her rocking chair, and sat in it. Her heart recognized a rhythm and pounded to a distant beat. A flash of drums crossed her memory, the same sound that often called her in the night and reminded her of the land of the people she descended from.

Despite her eighty years, Mama walked to the Mount Zion Church every Sunday. Those long treks of hers had turned the loose soil into a path of hard-packed, gray earth that ran to the main road. Mama considered herself a faithful Christian. She had been a member of Mount Zion for more than sixty years, before World War II. Most parishioners who had known her since she joined the church as a pre-teenager trusted her; others were wary of her. They were uncomfortable around her because she had "the gift." Nevertheless, she couldn't help how those people felt and she couldn't deny what was coursing through her body. Her instincts were acute. Oftentimes, she could look at a man and know he was up to no good before he even spoke. Grandma Dee had called it "the knowin' of what was comin'."

An old, white-haired preacher man with a smile on his greasy lips once told her he could cast out the demon in her with a few swigs of his wine, but she knew better. After a sniff of his clothes soaked with the cheap fruit of the vine he'd spilled on them, she backed off. With tears in her eyes, she told him, "Jesus left it in me to know a good preacher man from a bad preacher man." She shook her finger at him, "You ain't a good one. Jus' move along." He wasn't going to mess with her good thing. After all, she had "the gift." She reckoned Jesus wanted her to use it. "It don't make no sense for my Grandma Dee to teach me the good mojo if I was just to get rid of it. Lawd, I been saved to do good, and I'm gonna do it by usin' what I got!"

She blinked, trying to clear the tears, then she looked around. "Why is there so much light in this room?" She stared at the plastered walls covered with newspaper, held together with a mixture of starch and water. It closed the light from the cracks, so the rooms in the row house should have been dark. Mama looked at dates on those old papers and they triggered thoughts about her long life. She had seen a lot, her heart had hurt a lot, but she was patient. Instinct told her she had a purpose; something big was going to happen and she would play a part in it.

She sighed, because she sensed the moment she had been waiting on was soon coming to pass. She heard the churning Sunflower River call her name as it had for Grandma Dee so many years ago. When she started needing naps in the afternoon and her heart wasn't beating steadily like it used to, Mama didn't go to the doctor, she had no use for them. She chose to look up the symptoms on the fancy cell phone her daughter Tippiny sent her, a handy tool for a solitary lady. She could ask it questions, and it talked right back! One day she told it how she was feeling. The pleasant but distant voice diagnosed the problem as something called afib. All that meant to Mama was that her time was coming, but not yet.

"Oh, yes, dear Lord. There's a time and place for everything, like the Good Book says. She glanced at the wall calendar, another gift from Tippiny. Above the year 2012 plastered on the page was a picture of the Washington Monument in D. C., where her daughter worked part of the year for a law firm. The rest of the year she worked in Atlanta. *Such a nomadic life and no time to come see me. Will I see Tippiny again? Dear God, is this going to be my last year on Earth?*

Her bones creaked as she reached for her long willow wood stick. She wrapped her claw-like fingers around its knob, using it to pull up from her rocking chair with hands roughened from growing up picking cotton. Her knuckles tightened with the strain, but she managed to get to her feet. Straightening her back to her full five-foot height, she tucked loose strands of white hair into the braided twist at the nape of her neck. Then she buttoned up her gown over her ample bosom, smoothing out the wrinkles before she slipped on her rough-hewn sandals.

Staff in hand, Cheche made her way to the sun-bleached boards that served as her front door that she'd left open to catch the morning breeze. Rain poured harder, and she felt cool splatters of it on her arm. Not wanting to get wet, she pushed on the door to close it and the rusty hinges creaked. She stopped and rolled her dark brown eyes. The mojo was coming. The soft plop of water hitting the front porch had a haunting beat. "Oh, my it's callin' to me."

She shuddered as she struggled to open the door again feeling the need to go outside. She looked up at the high tin ceiling covering her porch, shielding her eyes from the glare, the strange bright light reflecting back at her. Water snaked its way through the edges of a hole in her porch roof, one that had been puttied up years ago. The round puncture had bits of tin flaring out from its center, jagged and sharp. Cheche used her stick to force the putty back in place. A memory she had avoided resurfaced; something from a very dark night in the Mississippi Delta. That bullet hole made her shake all over. She clamped her lips together and then smiled, "But I was clever to hide that proof in plain sight. Nobody's ever going to discover it."

The water from the edge of the hole appeared to run red. Cheche put her ebony hand under the flow and stared at what she saw as blood coursing over her hand. She then rubbed wet, blood-covered fingers through her curly hair, loosening the bun and causing thick drops to run into her eyes. She brushed the liquid aside. *This is a very powerful vision.* Memories flooded her brain. Her entire body vibrated. The memory became a vivid reminder of the day Goldie went missing. *This rain's gonna bring up the dead. Lordy, it's time for the dead to rise.*

Mary S. Palmer & Paula Lenor Webb

Mississippi Mojo ...and Murder

Tale of the Blues

Mary S. Palmer & Paula Lenor Webb

Chapter 1

Sheriff Hunter Harley spotted the red and blue lights from Deputy Rocconi's squad car as they flashed in the distance. In the thick darkness of midnight, those bright colors reflected off the torrid streaks of rain falling from the sky onto the pavement. Combined with the glow from the spotlight shining toward a scene of some sort of crime, the situation caused Harley to suspect he was driving toward a deranged rainbow. He moistened his lips. *What the hell is going on? Something serious.* He pressed his foot on the brake, taking a sharp left turn next to an abandoned gas station. His brain whirled as he thought about what awaited him when he reached his destination.

If a crime could have happened in the worst of places during the worst of times, this was it. The place was outside the jurisdiction of the City Police Department, so the Sheriff's Department had to take the call. The conditions were equally distressing. It had rained for weeks in Cleveland, Mississippi and everything was saturated. Mud and water filled up every creek, riverbed, and low spot in Bolivar and Sunflower County.

Delta State students who lived in the apartment complex on the outskirts of town during the summer term

3

made a game of the situation. They floated in inner tubes in the five-foot-deep water at their front doors. Others didn't venture out. More cautious, they knew that without a car or truck with four-wheel drive, it was safer to stay home.

Why now and why me? thought Hunter as he turned right onto an unnamed, unpaved road, trying to get closer to the scene without throwing more mud about with his patrol car. His back wheels spun in the slick mud. *Just nine more months here and I'll have a job in Jackson or Mobile.* He had left his home in Dallas, Texas three months ago to take this job. He expected it to be quiet, giving him time to recover. His unsolved serial killer case back in Dallas was almost the end of him. Failure had never been acceptable for Hunter Harley. He sighed, remembering the dark night when he stared at his service gun, thinking it was the only way out.

He didn't go through with the suicide, but he needed a change, and this appeared to be a good one. A small Mississippi town, no one knew his history, next to zero murder rate, and an easy job compared to the one in the big city. He sighed as he dodged a mud hole big enough to swallow his police cruiser. He sucked in his breath. *Is everything about to change? If blues music was born of bad circumstances, then I think I'm about to have one.*

Hunter had not anticipated how blues music and lifestyle it fostered had infiltrated and soaked into the bones of the Mississippi Delta. He considered himself to be one hell of a detective, but this local culture was way beyond his Texas-based understanding. However, it had its benefits, such as tempting food. He rarely passed by the local Delta Diner at lunch time without stopping. Once he went inside and got a whiff of chicken frying, he'd pass up other items on the menu to enjoy that fare. He had already let his belt out one hole to compensate.

However, his job was enforcing the law. He was grateful to Deputy Sheriff Zita Rocconi for walking him through some unexpected rough patches. Crime rates were low, but Cleveland had its share of unsolved mysteries. He soon discovered small towns have surprises if a person digs around a little.

He had not lived in Cleveland one whole week before he heard of the mystery of Goldie Parsons, the famous blues singer of the Mississippi Delta. It seemed that everyone else knew about this legendary bluesman. His one and only solo record was still a bestseller, the tune a staple for musicians today, and any first editions found in attics, basements, or estate sales made those who discovered one feel rich. Parsons disappeared in 1941--less than a month after he made that record--and was never seen again. Most people assumed he was dead since no trace of him had ever been found.

Goldie sightings came close to the number of Elvis sightings, and someone was always claiming to see the blues singer's ghost floating somewhere in the Delta. However, those witnesses had little credibility. They tended to be drunk, high on drugs, a toxic combination of both, or people with vivid imaginations who were always seeing things.

Hunter didn't buy into all of this speculation. This missing Goldie Parsons had probably been dead for decades. He could not help but wonder why the dead and the buried could not just stay that way. All the myth and mystery happened long ago. He took a deep breath. Now, with whatever was going on, chances were that things were going to be stirred up. Hunter had had enough of being the headlines. He still cringed whenever he Googled his own name to see what would flash across the computer screen. And he never liked what he saw. He came to this easy little town to escape that mess. Checking the battered watch he'd earned after being a cop for ten years in Texas, neon hands telling him it was fifteen minutes after midnight, he wondered what time had in store for him.

Hunter pulled up to another narrow, unnamed road in front of the old Tollar plantation, took a right turn just before the great oak tree, and passed the old cotton bin. He dodged the deep mud holes, but his car bounced around, splashing mud and water everywhere. Deputy Rocconi's squad car lights guided him to the bank of the Sunflower River like a landlocked lighthouse. He stopped next to her patrol car and saw her walking around with a flashlight's beam reflecting off the raging river below.

The rain came down harder. Hunter had encountered rainstorms like these back home, but they didn't occur as often as they did here. When he got the call,

6

he had settled for bed. No time to put on his uniform, so he slipped a t-shirt and Wrangler jeans over his pj's, then he grabbed his Stetson cowboy hat, the last vestige from his time in Texas, and pulled on his well-worn boots.

Deputy Rocconi saw him driving up in the distance and walked toward his car. Hunter could barely see the Sunflower River through the downpour, but he could hear it churning against its edges when he opened the door. An odor of damp and rotting vegetation filled the air. He heard water lapping against the pylons of an old pier. They'd been put there for boats to dock before reaching the Mississippi River. Taking in the scene amidst torrents of water falling from the sky, he gritted his teeth when he spotted the remains of a body, human bones to be exact, sticking out of the mud. He had not worked a night this bad in a long time. A memory of a similar case in Dallas flashed through his mind and he forced it away.

Yet, despite the chaos, Zita Rocconi appeared in her standard-issued mud boots, seemingly oblivious to these horrible conditions. Conservative in her attire and make-up, she always wore Opium perfume but never enough to be offensive or overwhelming. With a whiff of it, Hunter's thoughts were diverted from the crime scene for a moment. Of all the women he had been around, both in Texas and Mississippi, short of his mamma, Zita impressed him the most.

Tall and dark, the Italian blood running strong through her veins, Zita was tough enough to be an effective deputy. She helped him adjust to the Mississippi

Delta and its subtle ways more than any other officer might have done. Her connection to the community also aided him in getting answers when normal policy could not. In the Delta, an outsider stayed an outsider for life. Harley was fine with this since he planned to be in this town for only a year, but he was glad sad circumstances had turned lucky for him. He was hired to fill in after the sudden death of the longtime sheriff, Johnny Grimes, the son of Husk Grimes.

But he wasn't the first choice. The sheriff the townspeople of Cleveland, Mississippi really wanted was a local man, another member of the Grimes family, Richard Grimes. However, it happened that Richard, the "Chosen One," was unavailable since he was still in graduate school determined to finish his forensics training before going into service.

* * *

Richard and Harley had met at a field training exercise near Dallas and made a connection that turned into a friendship. When Johnny Grimes died, it was Richard, his son, who suggested that Harley take the job of sheriff until he, himself, finished training and could run for the position at the next election.

"Hunter, I know the town is small, and not what you're used to, but if you want it, I have influence with the Board of Supervisors and I can convince them to make you sheriff," he said when they sat at a bar drinking a beer one night. Richard knew the Dallas Chief of Police had given

Hunter an ultimatum: resign or else. That had left Hunter struggling with what to do and where to do it.

"This job as interim sheriff will be good for you. It's temporary, like you're looking for," Richard said. "When I am done with training, you will have some new experience. It's a little different there. You'll see the way police work in the deep South. When you learn our ways, you can work anywhere in Mississippi, Alabama, or Georgia." It sounded like the perfect situation for a man with nowhere to go.

* * *

Sheriff Harley braced himself for the steady downpour as he got out of the car and stepped into the deep mud. It covered his boots up to the silver buckles on the sides. He slipped on his Stetson hat and thick drops of rain ran down the brim of it. Uncovered parts of his shirt became soaked, allowing his hard muscles to show through the white fabric. Zita Rocconi looked at him, blushed, and glanced away. Hunter smiled as the chill from the shower ran down his spine as he walked over to where Deputy Rocconi stood.

Zita said, "I hated having to call you out on a night like this, but I thought you would want to see this for yourself. Have you ever heard the famous blues singer's story?" He looked at her. He could see the excitement deep in her brown eyes, but he also saw her struggle to stay professional. He nodded, realizing what story she meant--the story of Goldie Parsons. She was right. Like it or not, he needed to be here.

Trying to distract his thoughts from the macabre scene, he focused on Zita's hair and how it fell loose below her shoulders. Hunter liked it best that way, he could see the drops of rain running in little rivers through her thick locks and down her police-issued raincoat. The bright yellow of the slicker made her look like a beacon in the night. He narrowed his eyes. *So she suspects the same thing I do.* What laid at their feet, however, was no ghost, legend, or a product of Delta mythology. "Yes," he replied. "I know the story's been around forever, but I didn't think that so-called legend about Goldie Parsons was real." Hunter cocked his head.

"Neither did I...until now." Zita's spotlight beamed through the darkness and rested on a skull. Hunter didn't have enough forensics training to determine race from a skull, but he could tell it belonged to a male. What made this skull different from all others? He couldn't miss the one gold tooth shining up at them. Although it happened far in the past, the tooth brought to mind the signature always associated with Goldie Parsons, the famous missing blues man of the South.

"Who found the remains?" Hunter asked, hoping against hope it wouldn't be a local. If so, the town would know before the sun rose and the media would be alerted before breakfast. He glanced toward the nearby patch of woods by the dirt road that led to a bunch of old row houses, and other possible places someone might hide. He didn't want anyone there as his officers examined the crime scene.

"Three Delta State kids, out here on a dare. Can you believe it? They knew the story, only they thought Goldie was a ghost haunting the river. They came out here to see. Freaked out when they saw a femur bone sticking up out of the mud, they ran. They didn't even see the skull. I found it by looking around. The kids called 911 when they got back on campus." A hint of laughter infiltrated her voice. She focused her flashlight over to more bones near the skull.

"Do you think they associated the bones with the legend?" Hunter asked.

"Well, if they have not put the two together by now, they will soon. I would say we have a few hours to come up with something to tell the reporters. This is going to be big...really big. Kind of like finding Jimmy Hoffa big."

"Hopefully, it is Hoffa," the sheriff quipped back.

The driving rain made it next to impossible to uncover anything in the mud at their feet. "Sir, where do we start?" Rocconi stood in place as Sheriff Harley walked in the mud and surveyed the scene. He was glad she'd learned to watch and wait for him to answer her questions. She told him once, "I know when to keep my mouth shut. You deep thinkers need quiet moments to gather your thoughts and assess the situation and I admire you for it." It was nice to be understood.

Hunter looked down at the skull at his feet. Its empty sockets where eyes once were glared back at him demanding he find who did this. He watched a slight smile form on Zita's face and wondered if she realized her name would go down in history as one of the people who found the great missing blues man, Goldie Parsons, if these bones proved to be his. She probably wanted to call home and share the gossip but she would wait. A professional, her job came first. So she did her job and tromped all around the area searching for clues.

"Rocconi," he said, "we need to mark off a five hundred feet perimeter around the crime scene. This should cover the bank of the river and down into the water. Call the station; tell them to bring plenty of crime tape, and get Deputy Chan to come out here."

"Chan is going to be very excited to see this, Sir." Rocconi replied.

"Good, because Chan is going to guard the scene tonight. Do not say who we think the victim might be until he arrives. We have got to try to keep the word from spreading as long as possible. We also need to do our best to secure this scene and process it properly."

"Yes, sir." She turned and walked toward her squad car.

"Oh, and Rocconi," Hunter said.

She stopped and stared back at him, "Yes, sir?"

Hunter's face suddenly became tight. His lips formed into a straight line. Emerald green eyes shining in the lights, he told her, "Remember this, we are not only answering to the public in regards to this crime, if this is Parsons, we'll end up answering to history, I want it done right. Call the forensic office in Jackson. Tell them what we suspect and say we need a forensics crime team up here as soon as possible."

"Yes, sir." Zita vanished beyond the headlights.

Hunter walked back to the skull and stooped down, sinking his knee into the Delta muck.

What happened to you? Harley stared at the skull. He turned, allowing light from the spotlight to shine on the bones, giving him a better view. He heard Rocconi requesting assistance, her radio chatter indistinct in the background.

A slight beam of light shone on the skull resting in the Delta mud. A single, circular hole rising halfway out of the mud caught his eye. *Gunshot, very interesting.*

He then rose and walked around the skull, wondering what other remains might exist. The femur bone the Delta State students said they first saw poked up out of the mud like a cryptic flagpole. He then walked closer to the river, headlights from Zita's patrol car still filling the area.

Large rib bones, clearly belonging to the rest of the remains, glistened in the deep mud. It was a miracle they were still grouped together. Hunter walked to them, somehow churned up from their previous resting place. He bent closer for a better look. He could see a deep, circular scrape on the edge of the otherwise smooth area of the rib bone. *Another gunshot, right through the ribs.* It was clear this was a murder investigation.

Sheriff Harley stood and walked back to the skull. He stared at the vacant eyes and asked, *Goldie, if this is who you really are, who wanted you dead?*

Harley's heart skipped a beat. He would have sworn he saw a twinkle in the empty sockets where the eyes should be.

Chapter 2

One humid night in the Mississippi Delta, Eleanor Tollar opened the massive bay windows leading to her bedroom balcony. Located on the second floor, they were designed to catch the cool breeze that frequently blew across the Sunflower River running next to the family plantation. That plantation remained in the Tollar family for generations; it had been passed from father to son since before the Civil War. Originally a thousand acres of swamp and mud, her family tamed the land and made it grow rows and rows of cotton. Only this time there were not any sons left to leave anything to, only a daughter.

Despite the slight breeze, Eleanor's cotton house dress was soaked with perspiration trickling down from her armpits. She brushed a speck off of some tiny red roses on a background changing from deep amber to a brighter blush, depending on where the beads of moisture ran.

The dress was a "ready-made" her mother, Elma, brought back from her latest trip to Memphis. It was the only piece of clothing her mother bought that she liked. Eleanor would turn eighteen in December, so her mother was focused on her upcoming introduction to society. Her chiffarobe was full of all kinds of fluffy pink clothing. Ball gowns with large shoulder pads to make her look skinnier than she was hung on the rods, and lingerie designed to tuck and taper her body into a desirable shape filled her chest-of-drawers. Everything purchased suited her mother's sense of style.

The outfits Eleanor liked were shoved to the sides; her black, green, and gray Sunday dresses became hidden amongst the glitter. All of her other favorite items were moved from sight, even her books, like *Oliver Twist*. They were slipped into drawers, while silver hair clips and fashion magazines took their place. If she complained, her mother would say, "Act like a lady, Eleanor and read those modern magazines. Dickens is dead, honey, you need to focus on the living. Speaking of living, have you seen that Baker boy? He's grown into something handsome and his daddy is rich. I wonder how his mamma is doing? Eli told me she had a cancer scare! He also said Joe Baker was sweet on you. You need to talk to Joe at church next Sunday, I bet he would kiss you if you let him."

"I don't want him to kiss me, Mamma," Eleanor retorted. "And I wish you wouldn't listen to Eli Tarsi. He's a little goofy, a Mama's boy. Did you ever notice how he scribbles in that little notebook? What is he writing down? It makes me nervous. Why does he start his sentences with 'Mama says...?'"

Elma blinked and stiffened her back. "Well, he does good work for me and he'll do anything I ask him to.

That's more than I can say for my own daughter. Look how you toss aside the beautiful clothes I buy you. If I didn't insist, you wouldn't even accept your position in society. But I'm not going to let you ruin that opportunity for me...um, for you."

The planning for Eleanor's future started when her figure started to develop and the boys noticed. Elma hadn't paid her daughter much real attention until society friends commented on Eleanor's beauty. Then Elma saw an opportunity to bask in Eleanor's glory, and she took it. The Saturday before Eleanor's eighteenth birthday in December, she would be introduced to society at a fancy event held in her home, the Tollar Plantation.

Her mother set another goal, one to get her daughter wedded and bedded to one of the best families in the Mississippi Delta. Her mother told her, "It's time for you to find a husband, Eleanor, and you have to dress the part to do so. Men don't look at a plain girl." Since her husband unexpectedly died of a heart attack a year earlier, Elma's attention turned to improving her standing in the community and she planned on using her daughter to do it. Elma was also getting lonely and bored in the big house. So, she invited men friends to visit to keep her company.

Eleanor ignored her mother's complaints about her running around the plantation in plain dresses, even if they were a step up from the old button-down shirts and pants her daddy used to wear. She loved them because they still carried the scent of his aftershave. She wouldn't have even changed and stopped wearing his clothes then if it weren't for the black woman, Tippi Brown, who really raised her, insisting, "It's time to grow out of your childish foolishness; you need to be lookin' for a husband, Child."

When Mama Tippi said those words to her, she felt betrayed. It seemed everyone was turning against her, making her grow up. She didn't want to be responsible and married to some local boy. She wanted to go to college at Ole Miss and become a teacher, writer, or travel around the globe. She longed to escape her present world and its boring existence. She wanted adventure.

Today was tough. All morning her mother had harped at her. Those endless passive-aggressive comments set Eleanor's nerves on edge. *Wear this...stand up straight...don't blink so much...* Elma's words reverberated in her head...*Some daughters appreciate the advice their mammas give them.* Finally, Eleanor broke down and changed into the dress with roses flying all over it because it was the most comfortable of the new collection. Besides, it kept everyone from fussing at her, at least temporarily.

Eleanor leaned her shoulder against the white window frame and faced toward the cotton bin, just a few hundred yards away. She could hear the tuning and thumping of guitars.

Next came the stomping of feet along with the strumming. It came from some of the black field workers on the porch of the old cotton bin, singing songs only heard in this little piece of the world. It was what she liked about the Delta. The music carried clear up past the house and beyond, farther than anyone realized.

"I know my lady loves me..." came floating from the cotton bin, where her family had stored cotton seed for years.

The rich deep voice of one of the singers drifted through the night air. "Wylie Martin," she thought, "is back." A picture of him formed in Eleanor's mind. Of all the players on the plantation, the man was shortest in stature, but the loudest. Mr. Martin gave up working in the fields years ago for playing in juke joints and speakeasies and took to always wearing a blacksuit and a red tie. Nowadays, that suit might be worn a bit with the edges of those shoulder pads a little shiny from usage, but it was the nicest one he owned.

She cracked a smile. Her daddy loved to hear the blues musicians singing on a Saturday night, Wylie most of all. "If they work hard in the fields, Saturday night should be theirs," Daddy always said. But Mr. Martin got special treatment. When Daddy discovered Wylie was in the area, he would give Eli a dollar to find him and invite him to the Tollar plantation to play. He'd be allowed to stay in one of the row houses on the far side of the field and given twenty dollars in credit at the Joe Wang's Market in town. Daddy respected Wylie and insisted his daughter did, too. "Call him Mr. Martin, little girl," he told Eleanor, "he's earned it."

Eleanor knew Mr. Martin was fond of her daddy as well. The two men never exchanged the words acknowledging respect; it just wasn't done. Black was black and white was white. Race distinction wouldn't allow such an admission. Tollar did bend the rules by calling Wylie "Mr. Martin". Wylie accepted that compliment; aside from that, he didn't interact personally with her daddy, except in one case. Sometimes circumstances cause people to do unexpected things. When they buried her daddy in Magnolia Cemetery, she saw Mr. Martin, hat in hand, standing by the gate at the entrance, his way of displaying respect.

Yet, while many of the black minstrels of the Mississippi Delta tended to ride the rails - the Pea Vine they called it - and travel from plantation to plantation looking for work and playing the blues, Mr. Martin usually stayed at the Tollar plantation, often longer than expected. Nothing had changed since daddy died. Mamma knew the blues music kept many workers at their plantation, so she kept the same policy as daddy had. Although most other blues men would pick up and leave in four weeks or so, Mr. Martin kept on playing and teaching others out in front of the cotton bin. "He must be teaching tonight," she thought. It was rather quiet down there for a Saturday.

Eleanor was no stranger to the blues nor the bluesmen who sang them. She had heard their singing all her life. When she was younger, she used to climb the great oak tree next to the cotton bin and listen to their songs. On long delta nights, she would lay across her Daddy's lap, her head resting in the crook of his arm and bare feet dangling off the armrest. He'd tell her, "One day, my little darling, you'll be running this plantation." The rocking chair swayed backward and forward, speeding up or slowing down to the pace of the song being played. Her daddy would rock her to sleep to the sound of their rhythmic humming. She missed him so much on these nights.

As a little girl playing in the long cotton fields by the big house, she was mesmerized by the rhythmic, soul-stirring songs coming from the cotton fields. She watched their dark faces as they worked hard picking the cotton. The white cotton sacks grew from empty to full, and heavy, as they worked their way along the rows toward the house. They moved back and forth, up and down amongst the cotton stocks, dragging the nine-foot sacks behind them. It was laborious, back-breaking work but they kept on singing. During moments when they seemed miles away, she could hear one person start to sing about something and then pass by somebody else. If the mood fit how another man was feeling or thinking, he would join in and sing too, as he sauntered along. It was like a conversation, only they sang instead of talking.

Eleanor remembered hopping from one black dirt row to another, trying to keep up with the deep, rhythmic beat that seemed natural to the black sharecroppers who worked for her daddy. Even as a young girl, the old sounds touched her somehow.

"I knows my lady loves me..." she heard yet again.

She remembered when Mr. Martin first came on the plantation. He brought with him something different. His playing wasn't like the others. It was deep, and raspy, and stood on its own. "It's got the powa, the mojo," Grandmama Dee always said. "It creeps into yo' bones and makes yo' wannna sway to the music." Grandma Dee would know. She had taken care of her daddy growing up on the plantation just like Tippi looked after Eleanor during her formative years. Now, along came Cheche, Tippi's daughter, working around the plantation. Tradition abounded.

"But my lady, she lives with another man," she heard a voice sing from below.

Her daddy enjoyed the music. He let them play within earshot of the house, so it had to be okay, she thought. He would sit on the big front porch with the lights turned off and just listen. Sometimes Eleanor would sit with him, but not always. Her mamma did not agree; she thought black music was terrible and would busy Eleanor somewhere else if she felt like her daughter was getting too much exposure. Elma had fussed about the "noise" for years, but her daddy ignored his wife's complaints.

Mamma tried to hold one of her famous Delta tea parties on a Saturday night once, but only once. Eleanor Jane Toller remembered that night well. Momma made her wear her yellow Sunday School dress and black leather sandals. She was a little girl, maybe six-years-old, and restless. She remembered trying to slip outside, but Mama Tippi refused to let her out the door. "You gonna' get dirty!" she said with a pat on the bottom. Eleanor settled for dancing around the big table in the dining room and dodging the legs of those putting out mamma's best tea service.

The sharecropper wives, who were paid a little extra in-store credit to work the party, swayed to the tunes creeping up from the cotton bin into the living room while they dusted the tables. It was a chance for them to be in an unfamiliar, elegant area. The Tollar's spacious house on a wide acreage was a big contrast to the row houses the field workers and their families lived in. Those tiny houses sat in one long row down a dirt road, out of sight from the main house. They did not have any sort of yard, only rows of cotton growing up to the doorstep. Four cabins held everyone's family, including grandparents, aunts, and cousins.

They all picked cotton on the plantation. The men received fifty cents a day, the women forty. Since they were not sharecroppers, they got no part of the harvest. If they left, some member of the household had to continue to work on the plantation or else the family had to leave. Most wanted to work for her father, a southern aristocrat, but respected. No one denied he was a fair man.

During that party, though, different sounds crept in from outdoors, what Eleanor remembered the clearest was the words of her parents.

"John, they have to stop. My tea..." Mamma pleaded with Daddy.

"Elma, I gave them my word they could play every Saturday, and I will not break it. It also guarantees we have workers for the crops," he said firmly.

Elma opened her mouth to protest, but John raised his hand to stop her. Before she said another word, he walked out of the room, leaving her mother red-faced with anger. Elma never held another party on a Saturday.

A second voice, a new voice, brought her back to reality. He wasn't Wylie, but his music was good. It was different. It called to her through the Delta darkness. It was haunting, there was the normal strumming, and she could hear Mr. Martin's guitar backing up the lead, but then the other person sang.

"I have searched high and I have searched low," he belted out in his own style.

The power of the Delta blues wasn't in the words of the song, but in the power of the voice behind them. This man dragged out the line and his voice went so deep it dripped like Spanish moss on cypress trees. It was so alluring that it caught her attention.

"Who are you?" she wondered, looking through the darkness towards the only view she had of the cotton bin; the full moon shining on the rust-riddled roof of sheet tin and patch jobs where water leaked through. His voice was strong. It was so powerful. She had to know who he was. She leaned over the edge of the windowsill but could not see the porch of the cotton bin where they all were playing. It was near midnight, but she needed to get outside and hide behind the great oak next to the house where she could see the porch better.

Eleanor opened her bedroom door and looked up and down the hallway. She didn't want her mamma to know what she was doing. It had been this way since she turned seventeen and Daddy passed. Things had been tense between mother and daughter for quite some time, but the fighting became much worse without Daddy around to mediate and calm them down. Eleanor sneaked down the steps leading to the living room one at a time. They tended to crack, but she knew which ones to avoid and she did.

She got to the bottom of the stairs, then opened the screen door leading to the front porch and to the haunting voice that called to her. It was dark, lights already turned down for the night. She closed the screen door behind her and stopped for a moment.

"Miss Eleanor, "When the small child's voice spoke her name, Eleanor jumped. She could see Mama Tippi's little girl's ebony cheeks reflected in the light from the porch of the cotton bin. She saw the shine in the girl's eyes. Deep, haunting orbs that had a sparkle. Cheche was only ten years-old, but she acted mature. She was the strangest little black girl Eleanor had ever met. She never saw her playing with the other children on the plantation, only walking among the cotton pickers or drawing in the mud by the river. Other children asked Cheche what she was drawing, but she never replied.

Cheche was an old soul in a child's body. She was not able to explain why she got out of her nice warm bed at midnight, only that she had to. She would leave being curled up next to her mamma, safe and snug without giving a reason. Cheche was an honest child, who told the truth, but it was hard to believe her weird statements. "My bones itched," she often said in the airy voice of a child. But no more. That had to be enough to satisfy anyone's curiosity.

This time, she had simply moved away from the warmth of her mamma's body, slipped on her navy shift dress and walked out the front door, past her grandma's bed. She sauntered along the hard dirt path in front of the row house she shared with her mamma and grandma toward the big house. No sneaking or slipping out the door; she just got up and left. She walked around the rows of cotton in the field and ended up on the porch of the big house...waiting. When Miss Eleanor crept out the front door in the dark, Cheche grabbed the edge of her dress as she walked by.

"Che, girl, you scared me to death!" whispered Eleanor after feeling the light pull, trying to avoid letting anyone know where she was. *Of all the luck!* Would this child tell on her? Maybe she could talk Cheche into not saying anything to her mamma.

"Miss Eleanor, listen close," Cheche whispered. "This is your crossroads. Somethin' awful big is about to happen. The Lord showed me. The pain, it be deep, you gonna to die inside."

"I have searched high and I have searched low," that voice sang again. Eleanor was drawn to the man behind the voice. Goosebumps popped up all over her arms. Fear consumed her. She'd never felt like this before. She turned her head to listen closer.

Cheche took a step forward and tugged on the edge of Eleanor's dress again. "Miss Eleanor, please listen. This ain't good. It's death, I tell you."

"Che, what are you talking about?" she asked, still distracted by the singing. "I'm just listening to a man singing the blues." Eleanor walked past Cheche down the steps into the yard and ducked behind the great oak tree just outside the cotton bin.

Che followed and stopped right behind her. "You don' know, Missy. How you actin' gonna change things. It's gonna hurt a lot." She shook her head. "I know, but sometimes things are meant to be, don't matter how much you wish they was different. Like light, and stars, and love. My grandma tole me, 'Che, girl, there are things more powerful than the mojo. You gotta accept it.' I got the mojo; I know things. I can warn you, but I can't stop you. You gotta stop yourself." Eleanor was no longer listening. Cheche looked down, sighed, and then walked away.

"My woman, she don't want this blues singin' man." Eleanor peeked around the trunk of the oak.

Eleanor studied the porch of the cotton bin, a worn combination of boards and tin. The bin itself kept the cotton seed dry and ready to plant for the next season. She let her eyes drift to the old porch stretching from the main building about twelve feet and beyond to the wood paneled floor worn in various, unusual places. Places where the chairs of blues singers scraped as guitars were strummed, bare spots worn down by the tapping of shoes to a beat. Also visible were small dents in the wood from women who couldn't resist the music so they would trek up the steps and start dancing, their high heels leaving their mark. Eleanor smiled. Many people have been here before. This place was marked as special.

Tonight, though, there were only two men: Mr. Martin and the man with the haunting voice. Eleanor could overhear them talking man talk, but it was mixed with instructions. Mr. Martin cautioned his companion, "You want to start off slow and easy. Lure them in, you got the voice for it, then pick up the pace. You gotta shake that Alabama accent."

She stared at the other player. His appearance shocked her, because he looked white, but he certainly didn't play like a white man. He resembled Mr. Martin. Both of them had light, red hair. Yet, Mr. Martin had clear signs of being of a mixed race. She moved sideways but made sure the tree still shielded her from sight. Was this visitor like Mr. Martin?

The strumming resumed, the two men humming in sync, searching for the right rhythm. The moonlight sparkled on a small ring the stranger wore on his right hand. When Eleanor strained to get a better look at the guest, her bare foot got caught in a hole made from the knotting of the root. Wriggling free, she caught her toe on another root and stumbled from behind the tree into a pile of leaves at the bottom of it, landing on the ground in front of the men.

Surprised, they stopped playing. She heard the thump of their boots across the wood floor as they both ran to the edge of the porch and jumped down onto the grass, rushing to get where she lay curled up at the base of the oak. "Miss Eleanor, my what a surprise!" said Wylie, giving her a hand up.

Eleanor clasped his hand and eased to her feet. "A pleasant surprise, indeed," the other man said in a deep, magical voice. She turned to look into the bluest eyes she had ever seen. Through no will of her own, her gaze became fixed on them. She saw stars sparkling as she never had before.

Then she lowered her own eyes to see his broad smile, the glint of a gold tooth in the moonlight made goosebumps break out again. Eleanor swayed sideways. When the singer caught her and held her in his arms, she wilted and made no effort to budge. *I've never felt like this before. Could this be love? Is this what Che was warning me about?* No answer came to mind.

Chapter 3

When the wind blew hard across the miles of cotton fields, Sheriff Hunter Harley's room at the Shackem Up Inn, on the outskirts of Cleveland, tended to creak and shudder. On bright days, bits of light crept through empty nail holes and patch-up jobs on the roof. At times, when lying in the bed way too short for his long frame, he could see the boards in the pitch of the roof move and threaten to set loose and fall on top of him. Ending up in a place called the Shackem Up Inn in a small, but respectable, town taught the sheriff that his deputy had a bit of a devious streak.

"You want the Delta experience; you need to experience it all," Rocconi told him on the phone when he asked her to find him a place to stay. "Don't worry, Sheriff Harley, I know the perfect place and the food is good." He could swear he heard her giggle before she hung up. What she had found was a former sharecropper shack converted to a single room called the Pink Palace in the longest stretch of land he had ever seen. People said, "You could see your dog run away for ten miles!" when describing it. In the middle of that expanse stood a collection of lone row house shacks, converted into a hotel and blues-themed restaurant.

Rocconi had chosen one of them for his temporary home while he served as sheriff in this small Mississippi Delta county. She picked the pink monstrosity the owners lovingly called the "Pink Palace." The exterior was planked, worn wood; the color was probably red—once. The beat-up look was carried inside his palace, too. Truth be told, he couldn't complain too much. His room was cleaned regularly, and the food was way better than expected. But it annoyed him that he could not convince them to stop leaving a Moon Pie on his pillow every day or to quit stocking his small fridge full of RC Colas. He didn't like Moon Pies and he hated the RC's!

Harley almost never got in a hurry. That was true, especially this morning, after being awake till almost daybreak, he took his time getting ready for work. Deputy secured. An earlier text message from Chan indicated a few more cars than normal had driven by the old Tollar plantation, but not enough to worry about. Harley donned his uniform, Stetson hat, and a different pair of boots, since the ones from last night were still caked with mud. He pulled open the old plank front door, its edge digging into the floor, leaving scratches. Then, he pushed past the warped screen door that didn't keep flies from coming into his room. He tolerated the annoyance of those pests. Complaining wasn't an option. Why ask to have one thing fixed when so many other things were broken?

It was an area almost as flat as similar places in Texas. Across from his lone shack, he could see Highway 61 as it ran South towards Cleveland. The blacktop road literally faded into the distance from the North to the South. Cotton field rows could be seen across the way, a spattering of trees here and there, but all of it showed not much more than dirt.

He ambled down the rickety steps and walked towards the largest shack house on the property. It served as the restaurant during the day and a blues bar at night. It was where Hunter usually ate breakfast. Levenia Abrams, a lifelong resident of Cleveland and one of the best cooks in town, greeted him with a huge smile. "Hi ya, Sheriff!"

Before he had taken off his hat and walked to the lime green retro 1950's kitchen table by the window, she whipped from behind the bar with a tall mug of coffee, three creams, and two sugars. Her ample frame moved gracefully as she slid the mug on the table in sync with his laying his hat on it and pulling out the red speckled and chrome seat.

He gave her a sideways grin. "Thank you, Levenia. The usual."

"Coming up!" she replied and whirled back to the kitchen. He could already smell the cathead biscuits--so named because they are as large as a catfish's head-- baking in the oven. His mouth watered for them and the scrambled eggs that would be served with them.

While waiting for his order, his thoughts turned to the body. He felt confident about keeping the discovered remains quiet, especially since Levenia didn't seem to know. If she had, she'd have said something. One thing he had learned since coming to the little town of Cleveland, Mississippi, if you couldn't find the information you needed on the Internet, then check with Levenia Abrams; she'd have the answer.

People strolled in and out of the restaurant, enjoying their breakfast. No matter, Levenia soon had two massive biscuits and a pile of scrambled eggs in front of him. "Thank you, it looks wonderful as ever," he told her as he dug his fork into the eggs. He kept his eye out for new faces, reporters, and journalists from all over. No one yet, he decided, as he saw only the tourists that looked like ordinary people coming through.

He leaned back in his chair, sipping his coffee when he heard the ding of a text message on his cell phone. Not in a hurry, he kept his strategy running through his mind. What would be the first thing to deal with today? Another ding from a second text came. "Okay, this is it." Harley drew up his legs, resting the mug back on the table. Now a phone call, the theme to the old western, "Rawhide," as his ringtone. He glanced at his phone; Deputy Sheriff Rocconi was calling.

"Hello..."

She cut him off. "You need to get to the courthouse now." Deputy Rocconi's voice was frantic. "The Mayor is about to announce the finding of Goldie Parsons. The

33

word's out and this place is swarming with media. I told him it would be best to wait on you since you are the sheriff and the case is under investigation, but I don't know how long I can hold him back."

"I'm on my way." Hunter hung up the phone. "Damn, didn't even finish my coffee." He got to his feet and headed for the door. "Levenia, I have to go," he yelled towards the kitchen, turning heads of everyone in the room, "Sorry I can't stay to eat!" He dropped a ten-dollar bill on the table.

As he headed out the door, she yelled back, "No problem, Sheriff! Go get 'em!"

Seconds later, he was racing to the courthouse in his patrol car. He did not want to attract the reporters so he left his siren off. Another call came in, "Rawhide" chiming away. It was Zita again.

"Sheriff, you know the back way into the courthouse, right? The reporters don't seem to know about the old road by the First Baptist Church. Park at the church, come down the back way and go by the air conditioners. I will be waiting at the door."

He quickly replied, "Sure thing. Is it getting bad?"

"It isn't getting any better. The Mayor is waiting on your update," she said.

"Thanks, pulling up to the church now." He hung up.

He parked on the side of the First Baptist church and hid his car from the front of the old courthouse. He made his way down the one-car lane, behind some of the oldest homes in Cleveland. Up the street, he walked till he could see the back of the courthouse from behind the short growth of trees that lined the lot. He stepped out of the growth, looking left and right. The coast was clear for the moment. He could hear the chattering of a mixture of voices from the front of the building, imagining the chaos that loomed up there and what he had waiting on him. He moved toward a large metal-studded door, one installed to sneak out prisoners over a hundred years ago.

The irony was not lost on him. The Bolivar County Courthouse had a hidden door in the back. Built over a hundred years ago, with a small room on the fourth floor designed to hang convicted criminals, it provided a place to get a prisoner out of town and avoid a mob. Today, it would be his way into the courthouse.

Looking around a large oak tree near the front, he saw several major channel news vans, reporters, and onlookers from the community. All were trying to find out what was going on.

They still had not seen him. He tipped his hat low and walked in the shadows of the oak he had just hidden behind. Slow and easy, but it was not hard to get to the building. They all were focused on the grand turn of the century front doors, waiting on word from the Mayor.

He slid behind the row of rusting air conditioning units to the door they showed during tours of the courthouse and where it led to the hanging room on the fourth floor. He knocked once, paused, then once more. The door cracked open, Roconni's brown eyes peeked out.

"Glad to see you, Sir," she said.

"The word got out, hmm?" He smiled. "What is the condition of the crime scene? Still secure?"

"Yes, sir. We got extra help this morning. They just beat the new vans. Mayor Willis is getting ready to make an announcement."

"About what? All we got is a bunch of bones by the river. We have not identified them yet." He navigated the narrow hallways and worked his way toward the front of the building to the area where they normally held the important press conferences.

In the front foyer with its marbled floors, an impressive chandelier and spiraling double staircase, he found Mayor Willis standing in front of the main podium.

He was a sight! In less than twelve hours, the Mayor had managed to find out about the crime scene and dress in his best white Sunday suit. He was pulling away as his teenage daughter tried to powder the sweat running down his face and with his wife trying to smooth what little hair remained on his almost bald head. When he spotted the Sheriff, his eyes widened into round white marbles, and he said in a loud voice, "Oh Sheriff! The victim's Goldie, isn't it? Finally! Oh, think of it! We found him!"

"Wait a minute, Mayor." Harley held his hand up. "Slow down. First, we didn't find anything conclusive.

My deputy was the one who first arrived in that terrible weather last night after getting that call from those Delta State students. I arrived after her." He curled his lip. "I don't remember seeing you out there in that mud in the pouring rain." Then he continued, "Second, we do not know if it is Goldie. It could be him...or a drunk who fell in the river...or a criminal who escaped Parchman Prison. It's your call, Willis, but be careful. If you want to go in front of the media and risk showing yourself to be a fool, you can."

Looking deflated, then worried, the Mayor poked out his bottom lip. "Sheriff, the media is chomping at the bit. We have to say something. What do we tell them?"

"You should have thought about that before you called them, Mayor," he replied.

"I didn't call them! Channel 6 woke me up this morning asking me if it was Goldie Parsons. By the time I got dressed and to the courthouse, news vans were setting up in the front. When I got a call from the Nashville Paper wanting a quote for the morning edition, I knew it was out of my hands."

"The site has been secure since we found it last night. It could have been those Delta State kids talking. Right now, all we have are bones of a dead man." Harley clamped his hands together to keep them from shaking and showing how nervous he was. The courthouse doors were still locked, but the crowd of reporters was waiting on the other side. He could see the outline of their heads and bodies through the frosted glass.

"Okay, Harley," the Mayor said, "you take in the scene."

Harley took a deep breath and reminded himself this wasn't Texas, this was Mississippi. He was having flashbacks. The last time he had to deal with the media, it went badly. Now he knew what he was doing. This case didn't involve a serial killer. Plus, he didn't have to explain the death of children. He had to prove, or disprove, the identity of a man dead over six decades ago. He could do this.

"Now, let's make this happen. Mayor, your only job is to introduce me. I will take over from there answering questions. I can handle the reporters. You need to stay calm and say nothing about it being Goldie Parsons because we do not know who it is yet. Understand?" Harley told the mayor and the deputies that now surrounded him. "We will keep it simple. Let in the reporters, I will answer a few of their questions and then we politely usher them right back out the front door. If they want to camp out in front of the courthouse and wait for more details, fine, but not in here."

"Yes, sir," everyone replied, respecting his authority.

"Rocconi, I need you up here with me, on my right side. Mayor, stand to my left."

"Yes, Sheriff." She stepped up to the platform and the Mayor took his place on the left.

The lobby of the Cleveland Courthouse stood large and imposing on a plot of land in the center of the town that surrounded it. It lacked the massive porticos of similar courthouses, but its rectangular shape was impressive. Two deputies walked up to the large front doors and one turned the huge lock. The soft click of the release was the signal for reporters to pour into the lobby, followed by their cameramen, and anyone else struggling to be first to break the story. They filled the lobby to capacity. Harley could just make out locals streaming in towards the back, here to find out what the big deal was. Was that Levenia he saw just beyond the door? They had no chairs, so behind the curtain, through a small hole, Harley could see the crowd shift and sway from one foot to another, vying to get the best position. Waiting eagerly for everyone to step out.

"Okay, everyone, let's go." Harley took in a deep breath and stepped out behind the Mayor, Rocconi on his heels, both still in their assigned places.

The audience became hushed but continued to vie for the best position as the Mayor stepped forward to the microphone.

"I would like to thank everyone who came here today under these unusual circumstances. I am the Mayor of Cleveland, Mayor Willis. I have with me Sheriff Hunter Harley and his Deputy, Zita Rocconi. I..."

Harley gently tapped the Mayor on the shoulder, out of sight of cameras. "I...would like to bring Sheriff Harley up to answer your questions." Harley tipped his hat towards the Mayor as he stepped forward. He now stood as the focus of all the reporters.

Beads of sweat ran down Harley's neck. So much like before, but not. It is not the same, he kept reminding himself. A camera flash brought him back to this moment. "Hi, everyone. Welcome to Cleveland, Mississippi. I know you're here because you heard that we found the remains of the famous blues singer, Goldie Parsons. We did find remains next to the Sunflower River, but we have not identified them yet. As you know, it has rained a lot lately and some of our Delta State students were down by the river late last night and found those remains. They called the police and Deputy Rocconi was the first on the scene, then she called me. Right now, the scene is secure and waiting for forensics to come up from Jackson."

"It is too early in our investigation to make a determination. I will do my best to answer your questions, but as I have said, it's just too soon. I am afraid some of you made the long drive for nothing. What can I try to answer?"

A striking blonde reporter with piercing eyes used her hips and cleavage to work her way up front, holding up her hand first, Harley pointed in her direction, "Sheriff," she asked, "When did you first learn about the crime?"

"My deputy, Rocconi, called me last night and I came to view the scene. As I said, we have already placed a call to Jackson to get their forensics team up here. They are on their way."

A male reporter tucked his white dress shirt into blue pants, and when Hunter nodded his way, he asked, "Do you think it is Goldie Parsons?"

Hunter replied, "I can't say. I have been sheriff here for a short time and I really do not know much about Parsons. I am sure my team will catch me up soon. Now I am just concerned with identifying the remains. To help us make the process faster, please assist my people by not disturbing them while they are working the crime scene and, if someone gives you a tip about who this person could be, Goldie Parsons or someone else, please contact us right away. We want to notify the next of kin as soon as possible." He looked at his watch, "I can take one more question."

Hunter saw a woman standing in the back, dressed in all black, with dark eyes staring in his direction. They'd crossed paths before and it hadn't been pleasant. He recognized her as Jenny Stein, a stringer for the Associated Press.

"Sheriff," she asked in a sexy voice, "Do you think this is the same as your case back in Texas? The one with the child serial killer that you couldn't solve. Is that why you left and... "

Hunter knew it was coming, but it was hard not to show emotion. To avoid more interrogation about that case, he interrupted. "No, it is not the same. Thank you, that is all."

Hunter stepped back from the podium and walked to the side. Jenny, who freelanced for whatever papers would accept her stories, acted like a national TV anchorwoman. He knew that wasn't the last he'd see of her. She'd follow this and dig at him about not solving that case in Texas pointing out how the wrong man was convicted of the crimes. She'd stress that an innocent man spent a year in jail before they disproved his guilt. Jenny wouldn't let that go. She'd hang around until her big moment of revelation came to pass and she could bask in the limelight.

"What a bitch!" Rocconi commented as she followed behind him. "Thinks she's a big shot in that skin tight skirt and those four inch heels."

Looking over his shoulder, Hunter nodded. "Pegged her, didn't you? You sure got that right."

Mississippi Mojo... and Murder

Chapter 4

Dreamy-eyed and almost in a trance, from the brief encounter the night before, Eleanor recalled the few words she and Goldie Parsons exchanged after he picked her up at the great oak. It had ended with his promise, "I will see you again, Girl. How about meeting me back here at 8:30 tomorrow night?"

She nodded, unable to speak. The warmth of his hand caused hers to tingle. Eleanor returned to the house no longer concerned about the slamming of the porch door or the creaking stairs. As she entered the house, she completely missed the outline of her mother's frame in the dark by the kitchen door, but her mother didn't pay much notice. Elma was very drunk and not alone. She, too, had secrets to keep.

The next day as she walked home from town a few miles away after running errands for Elma, anything to get out of the house, thoughts of the night before absorbed her. This day was different, though. Last night had changed her view of life. When she passed by Joe Wang's Market off the main street, she took a long, hard look at the group of black men and women gathered there and stopped. For the first time, she really *saw* them. It wasn't like Mamma had always said, people didn't have to be separated by color. Black men and white men could get along if they could just get past themselves. Her daddy taught her how people could do that if they tried.

Recognizing some of the men from her plantation, Eleanor walked over to where they sat on old flour barrels lining the front of the store. All had on overalls in various shades of faded blue covering short-sleeved button-down shirts underneath. Despite the hats they wore to protect their heads from the hot July sun, their skin glistened from perspiration. When she approached, one man mopped his forehead with a red bandana he pulled from his pocket.

They chatted loudly in a dialect of their own. She understood some, but not all. The closer she got, the quieter the group became, and then they all turned to stare at her. "Mornin', Miss Eleanor," one man spoke up, "somethin' we can do for you?" It was the man she recognized, he and his wife were pickers in her daddy's fields.

"Sorry to disturb y'all's conversation, but I just wondered if you'd seen Mr. Parsons. I, er, heard him singing last night and I wanted to tell him how much I enjoyed it."

Another man slid off his barrel and stepped closer. "You mean that new man? Nome, I'se been here all day; I ain't seen 'im. He's a mulatto; thinks he's a bit better'n the likes of us, I reckon. The only thing he picks is that guitar. Seems like someone told me he's from Alabama. Talks funny, too. Like he's uppity or somethin.'"

Eleanor took a deep breath. So, her suspicions were confirmed. The man with the gold tooth was black. "Thank you for your time," she said as she walked away swallowing hard. She could hear them whispering among themselves as she left the group before they could see the disappointment in her face, but she had made a decision. *It didn't matter, it really didn't matter.*

***

With a child's curiosity, Cheche had followed Eleanor since she left the Tollar Plantation and she'd witnessed the exchange at Joe Wang's from across the field as she hid in the shadow of an oak tree. Her eyes widened as she saw Eleanor approach the black field workers, a dangerous interaction in the Delta. Eleanor had naively risked her reputation and the lives of those men. Eleanor's body movements and the mojo gave Cheche a chill. She could sense that Eleanor was seeing another side of life, different from the one in which she'd always existed. But she couldn't put a name to this shift.

"Mama, what is going on?" Cheche asked that evening when she shared what she witnessed to her mother and grandmother. She knew they had the answers. Grandmother had spiritual sense, but Mama had common sense. Her eyes could see beyond normal conception to things everyone else could only visualize in deep, quiet moments. Mama was the precept of truth, justice, and humanity in a world that lacked all three.

Mama nodded three times. "Miss Eleanor is starting to see things differently," she replied. They ended the evening on their row house porch, Cheche leaning against one of the hand-hewn posts. Her mother and grandmother sat in their rocking chairs across from her, the floorboards creaking with each rock of the chair. A single lightbulb in the front kitchen provided a shimmer of light from within the house.

Cheche gave a cockeyed grin, excited she had figured something out. "I know why. Last night, I saw Miss Eleanor fall and Mr. Parsons picked her up. Didn't put her down too quickly, either. Oh, Mama, you shoulda seen the look in her eyes."

"Yeah, Chile. You know, I practically raised Miss Eleanor. That lovelorn look was still on her face this mornin' when I was at the house cooking breakfast. It sure was." She shook her head. "I'm worried. Them two together ain't gonna work for most people. No, sir. All I know 'bout this Mr. Goldie Parsons is he rode in on the Pea Vine and took up practicing singing and playing with Wylie Martin. Oh, they both wonderful blues players, but I'm afeared Martin done sold his soul to the Devil, like Mr. Johnson. Changin' from gospel music to blues. You see how he ended up, dead by poison! Yes, he has. I ain't so sure if Parsons might do the same." She scratched her cheek. "'Sides, he black and she snowy white—that ain't no good match up."

Cheche picked at the ragged edge of her dress and sighed. Her body trembled when the mojo kicked in. All that Mama said Cheche already knew in her bones. No matter, she didn't control fate. Love has no boundaries.

There wasn't one damn thing she could do to change the situation.

Chapter 5

The lazy days of summer passed faster than Eleanor liked. She didn't want to finish her senior year in school. She didn't want to attend the Debutante Ball her mother had planned in December, either. Meeting Goldie turned the sad days after the death of her father into those filled with hope and promise for the future, one with Goldie.

After their first encounter in July, they met almost every night under the great oak and in two weeks, they'd developed a powerful connection. Speaking with a white dialect he said he'd cultivated on his own so he could go to Mobile and pass for white, he told her stories of Alabama, his family at Mon Louis Island, and his Creole heritage. Seeing Goldie, talking to him, being held in his arms and kissed while he told her about his travels was like an addiction she couldn't shake. Was this love or was she desperate to be free?

Even in her childlike naivete, Eleanor realized she may not know the difference. She didn't know what to do. She liked Goldie, but did she love him? Was this what people called "deep in the bottom of your heart" kind of love? While Mamma was sulking somewhere in the back of the big house, at dusk, Eleanor slipped outside the front door and sat on the porch steps. Pondering the issue, she wished her daddy were here. She could almost see him walking up to her from the fields as he did in the past. Much more tolerant and understanding than her prejudiced mother, he would understand, and he'd probably know the answers to her questions about life and love. She closed her eyes. She could hear Mr. Martin strumming his guitar, probably at the cotton bin practicing, and the tune carried on the wind soothed her.

That boy, he done met a girl,

Yeah, that boy, he done met a girl.

Love it be blind, his head's all in a whirl.

Love is blind, hmm? She wondered about that and about how Goldie felt about her? No matter if he said, "I love you," with every other breath whenever they met, and told her, "You're the light of my life, my star." It was so confusing. He would talk as if they were going to be together forever one moment and then carry on about hopping a train to Memphis the next. But he did take her face into his hands and plead, "Come with me, El, darlin'."

Eleanor Tollar made it clear to Goldie that she was not going to hop a train anywhere. She wasn't going to just go traipsing off like he wanted. Her mamma was intent on arranging her debut into society. Planning on it, dreaming of it. How could she just run away and expect her mother to understand and accept her actions?

Then there were Goldie's dreams. He was obsessed with making a blues record. He told her about the life of a bluesman, a solitary life that didn't include her, no matter what he claimed. El remembered the faraway look in Goldie's eyes when he mentioned meeting a celebrity. "I may get a break, El." His voice cracked as he used the nickname he had for her. "Last week, a man recording songs in the area, Mr. Alan Lomax, drove up to the cotton bins here at the Tollar Plantation to enlist Mr. Martin to play his songs. Then Mr. Lomax asked me to play. I pulled out my guitar and played the song *Reelin' Feelin'*." A wide grin exposed his gold tooth. "Mr. Lomax liked it. Yeah, I might get a big chance to go to Memphis and cut a record." His mouth made a straight line. "O' course, it mighta just been talk."

Sitting on an old cypress log on the edge of the Sunflower River, El scooted closer and patted his hand. Scraps of paper with notes jotted on them filled her lap. She was entranced with the song they'd worked on together, but the morose tone depressed her. She didn't mention how she felt to Goldie. No need to discourage his dream. Instead, she held up a sheet of the paper. "I bet this song called to Mr. Lomax just like it did to me. You'll hear from him, sooner or later." She shuddered as the words echoed in her ears:

I got this feelin'

It got me reelin'.

The logic behind the song was a strange happening they both shared. She told him about Cheche and her cryptic warning just before they met, about a relationship that would be dangerous. Goldie had a similar experience, only it was Grandma Dee who warned him.

"Miss Eleanor got you reelin' boy" Grandma Dee said when she met me after practice with Wylie, and she told me 'Get your house in order, cause it gonna be over.' He shook his head. "Honey," he whispered in her ear, "this is the mojo working and it makes me nervous."

Eleanor kept silent. She didn't believe in such things. But she didn't say so. She just shrugged. She didn't know all the answers. This was new to her. She was seventeen years old and Goldie was twenty. She knew Goldie wasn't ready for a commitment. Neither was she, but the feelings were so real and strong. *Is it wise to make plans when neither of us is ready?* She didn't want to lose her heart to him, but what if she already had? Could she go with him to Memphis? No! Her mamma spent a fortune with big plans for her debut. *I can't disappoint my mamma— can I? Maybe the real question is which one of us is willing to sacrifice our dream.* But it was her mamma's dream for her to find a rich man and get married in the Delta, not hers.

The way she was thinking was silly and dangerous. Despite logic, she kept having a dream that she and Goldie would run off and get married, to Memphis or someplace, buy land and settle down. It was nice, but she knew better. A black man was still a black man in the Delta - didn't matter how much white was in his blood. *A white girl with a black man is a sin.* It was best to stay away from those thoughts. Safer for everyone.

Another problem filled Eleanor's thoughts: Goldie was a blues singer. He was gifted, no doubt. Mr. Martin was only marginally better than him playing the guitar, And the songs Goldie put together with music meant something to her and anyone who listened. He had a future singing the blues.

Eleanor wondered if Wylie was the jealous type. She didn't think so, but anything was possible. Goldie was a viable threat. It didn't matter where he performed—on street corners, in juke joints, or on plantations, Goldie always drew a crowd. It was in his blood to follow his calling and he felt his chance was coming. He told her as much in their clandestine meetings.

It did. Two weeks later, summer was almost over and the hint of fall was in the air; things started popping. They had not met the night before since Goldie was playing at Jimmy's Juke Joint up in Belzoni. Eleanor had not expected to see him at all that week, since he was playing all over the Delta. For once, the house was quiet. Her mamma was up all night drinking with some man Eleanor didn't know and his sneaking out earlier that morning woke her up.

Too angry to go back to sleep, Eleanor dressed and went down to the kitchen to make coffee. She missed Goldie so much. The grandfather clock in the hallway chimed six times. *Too early to think such things,* she thought as she walked out the kitchen towards the front door. Daylight peeked in through the lace curtains, and to her shock, so did a pair of blue eyes.

Goldie's eyes met hers and he yelled through the door, "El, come out, Mr. Lomax has arranged for me to go to Memphis to record my first record!"

El threw open the front door and pushed open the screen door, slapping it hard against the side of the house. She rushed into his arms as Goldie snatched her up to kiss her. "Praise the Lord, my day has come. I'm going to be a star! My songs will be on the radio. Yippee!"

El's eyes darted towards the door; happy her mother wasn't around to see the show, she hugged Goldie back. For once, she was glad Elma was passed out drunk in the back of the house. She was thrilled for Goldie, but her heart was hurting. She wasn't as elated as her boyfriend, knowing mamma would never let her go with him. She didn't want Goldie to leave her. But could he give up that opportunity for her? Would she let him?

Tension escalated and Eleanor had no time to dwell on making a decision. The front door left open, allowing a hungover Elma to see her daughter and Goldie embracing. In uncontrolled anger, dressed only in a pink, silk nightgown, Elma flew through the open door and appeared before a startled couple. She snatched Eleanor from Goldie's arms, and dragged her back towards the house yelling, "You stupid girl. Idiot! What in the hell do you think you're doing?"

Elma managed to pull El off her feet, causing her to stumble, as she held her in a vice-like grip. She then swung El around like a ragdoll and shoved her daughter against the open door, her head jerked as it connected with the metal latch with a thud. When she crumbled to the floor and didn't move, Elma stared down at her and screamed, "No damn black man's going to take you off with him. Not as long as I'm alive."

Chapter 6

The next morning, Eleanor awakened feeling groggy. The bed creaked as she reached over to the nightstand for her watch to check the time. Not fully awake, her hand flailed through the air. *Where's the nightstand?* She shook her head to clear it and then checked the bump on the left side. It hurt when she pressed long brown curls covering it into her scalp. A warm hand touched her arm causing it to tingle; it was Goldie's. Her mouth hung open, but she didn't speak. In the silence, and everything from the day before replayed itself in her mind.

Eleanor remembered her mamma storming out the front door, dressed in her nightgown. She shook at the thought of that moment. *I've never seen Mamma in such a rage.*

Next, Eleanor recalled being slammed against something hard. Everything went dark, but she still heard the obscenities her mother screeched at her. Eleanor's greatest fear had happened, Elma found out about Goldie. Some of the words her mother used she'd never heard before. One statement stuck in her mind, "You've ruined all of my plans, you ungrateful brat."

She heard Goldie's steps on the porch as he dashed up to rescue her. Without a word, she felt him lift her from the floor asking, "You alright, Baby? You're safe now."

Goldie ignored Elma's protests as he took El into his arms and vaulted down the steps to the waiting car that was still running.

Eleanor's vision cleared and she watched Elma follow behind, but her mamma dropped to the ground as she tripped on the hem of her gown. Her fall didn't stop her objections. "You stop right now, or I'll sic the police on you!" she screamed in a slurred voice as she stumbled to her feet.

Goldie tossed Eleanor into the open rag top of Wylie Martin's 1938 Ford and then he hopped into the driver's seat. Elma was too late to prevent Goldie from flooring the gas pedal and driving away from the scene. So, Mamma was left shaking her fist as Goldie whisked Eleanor away.

"Your head hurt, darlin'?" Goldie asked as they headed for Hwy. 61. "I'll get some ice and aspirin." They stopped at Joe Wang's Market since it had just opened for the day. He went inside while she waited in the car. He came out with a couple of Cokes, ice in his handkerchief, and two asprin in his hand. "Put this ice on the sore spot and take a couple of these aspirin."

She washed the aspirin down with a sip of Coke. Then she rested the icy handkerchief on the bump. "It feels better, but I don't." Tears trickled down her cheek. "Mamma was so mad. She hates me now." She rested her chin in her hands. "Maybe you better take me back home, Goldie. The sooner I make things right, the sooner we can get past this horrible day."

Wide-eyed, he glared at her. "Take you back to more abuse? No way! You my woman now and I'm gonna take care of you. You can bet on that." He leaned over and kissed her on her wet cheek. "You're the light of my life. I got you and I ain't giving you up for nobody." He looked in his rearview mirror to see a patrol car passing by. "Uh, oh! I think a police car's coming." He scrunched down in the seat, hiding from view.

"Look, I know about Mamma's escapades with men and drinking. But Mamma wouldn't send the police after us. She doesn't want the attention," Eleanor told Goldie. But the little girl part of her heart wished her mother cared about her welfare, even if it meant a chase by the police.

"Mad as she was? She sure would." He sat up when the patrol car passed, started the engine and made a sharp right turn onto the highway. He kept his driving slow and easy till he was out of town. When he reached the main road headed North, he picked up speed.

El frowned as they whizzed by farmland. "I'm lost. Where are we going, Goldie?"

"Memphis, like I planned. Only thing different is I now got my lady by my side. I gotta meet the big man there and cut my record. He's got a hotel room for me, " He looked at her and winked. "I mean us."

El stiffened. "Goldie Parsons, I'm not staying with you in any hotel room. I believe in marriage and…"

He didn't let her finish. His blue eyes met her brown ones. "First comes marriage." His crooked grin exposed the gold tooth and El caved. "My buddy gave me the address of a Justice of the Peace outside Tunica. I didn't know I was gonna need it this soon, though." He rubbed his chin. "My friend told me that JP ain't particular about rules and regulations, or even marriage licenses. He'll let me check white on that form, too, I betcha. Goldie ain't my birthin' name, but it will be from now on. He won't ask." He held out a ten-dollar bill. "Especially if I hand him this." No traffic was on Highway 61, so Goldie pulled over on the dirt shoulder, snatched El into his arms and kissed her hard. She didn't resist. When he turned her loose, she was limp and her head hurt. "Now," he said, "Tell me that you'll marry me."

All El could do was nod.

They found a grassy area shaded by a small gathering of oaks and both got out of the car. He took her into his arms, hugged her close, and kissed her. Then he reached into the back seat and produced a brown paper bag. "Ta, da! My lunch and I'll share it with you, the light of my life." They sat on the grass; Goldie shared one of the homemade biscuits he took out of the bag. Then he removed waxed paper from two slices of pound cake, gave one piece to El and ate the other in three bites. Alternately, they took sips of an RC Cola as they watched a farmer plow his field in the distance. When they finished eating, he said, "Be back in a minute." He returned with his guitar and started tuning it. "I've got a surprise," he said. "I wrote this song for you and it's going to be on the flip side of my record."

You're my light, my star

I see you sparkling from afar

You're my life, my light, my star.

You're my day, my night

My world fills up with your silvery light

You're my life, my light, my star.

My light, my star, oh, I love you so

You're the one, I know

No other love is so sweet and pure

It's you, I am sure.

When I've got the blues

Your twinkle gives me a whole new view

You're my life, my light, my star.

No time or space can keep us apart

You have won my heart

I need you, woman, right next to me

Oh, with you I'm free.

Well, for me you'll shine

From here and now 'til the end of time.

You're my life, my light, my star,

You're my life, my light, my star,

My light, my star.

El flung her arms around Goldie, ignoring the remains of the RC Cola which poured onto the ground when she knocked it over. "Oh, Goldie, that's beautiful, so beautiful. It's the most gorgeous song I've ever heard." Her eyes lowered. "And you wrote it just for me."

"I meant every word of it, darlin'." A crooked grin crossed his mouth as he stood. "We'd better be on our way. Time to hop the broom! as they say back home. " He chuckled. "But we can't do that here. We will do it later, when it is just you and me." He shook his finger at her. "You'll always hear me speak like whites when I'm around white folks. But understand I've gotta talk the talk around my own folks, they're going to know I am passing." He tapped his cheek. "This Creole skin helps. Besides, lots of people don't care one way or the other in Memphis. I want to be a blues singer, but I love you. I'm not going to let this mess with the best parts of my life."

About an hour later, they pulled up to a mission-type bungalow holding hands, but El noticed it wasn't a courthouse. The faded sign saying Justice of the Peace stood cockeyed leaning against the front steps, hinting at the off-the-books activity within. Goldie rapped on the door. El was unsure if this was right, but she had made her decision.

A frumpy white woman of about sixty in a wrinkled skirt with a yellowed white blouse cracked the door. "Can I help you?" she asked.

"I hope so," Goldie responded. "We want to get married."

Her somber face broke into a smile. The door opened wider. "Come in. I'll get my husband; he's the Justice of the Peace." She cocked her head. "It's five dollars."

Goldie nodded, slipping her the ten. She tucked the bill into her bra as she left to get her husband.

Two golden-eyed cats, one black and one yellow, pounced into the room, jumped on different well-worn chairs, and ended their romp by curling into a ball on the window sill. El looked at the grime all around. No white dress or rose petals at this wedding. She wished they were in a church with friends and family. She bit the corner of her lip. *Mamma would hate this; she'd have a fit.* She was still dizzy, but Goldie spotted her wavering and caught her arm.

"Everything's gonna be fine, darlin'. Don't worry." He pointed to her head. "You okay?"

His smile rejuvenated her. "I am. Where's that Justice of the Peace? Get him in here and let's do this and leave."

A portly white man entered in a tight fitting sports jacket, the buttoned front straining against the seams, and an open-necked white shirt. In a deep southern drawl, he stated, "I'm ready, you two. First off, you have to fill out these papers."

The Justice stood over Goldie as he filled out the documents, including "White," as race, and El's age as eighteen. He handed them back completed, evoking a nod and a "Thank you."

A child could have memorized and performed the ceremony which lasted less than five minutes, ending with, "I pronounce you man and wife. You may now kiss the bride."

They kissed and were on their way with El praying the hotel would be a sight better than the JP's residence. She wasn't up for another shock on her wedding day. In an instant, everything had changed. For her, this was the beginning of a new life with a new name and a new husband.

The Welcome Arms Hotel, on a side street in Memphis, did appear to be clean, but it had no elevator. Relieved when the clerk who registered them didn't question Goldie's ethnicity or her age, El became concerned because the porter who escorted them to the third floor stumbled. When he turned around, she smelled liquor on his breath. They had no luggage, but Goldie slipped the porter two quarters. As soon as the man shuffled out of the room, Goldie pulled out a twenty-dollar bill. "Here, honey," he handed it to El. "Maybe this'll buy you a dress and me a clean shirt. Whatcha think, Baby. Wanna go shoppin' after a while?"

El didn't feel like shopping, besides, half of that twenty wouldn't buy anything she was accustomed to wearing. So, she declined, telling him, "I'd rather take a nap. Maybe that'll make my head feel better." She held out her hands. "Take off your shirt and give it to me. I'll wash it."

Her eyes were dreamy. Neither of them went shopping. The lumpy bed wasn't too uncomfortable. They wouldn't have noticed if it had been.

***

A voice brought El back to reality. "How're you doing, honey? Head better, I hope?" Goldie's kiss made her wide awake. Thoughts of yesterday vanished.

She rubbed the sore spot. "I think the swelling's gone down. It's still a little sore, though."

He took her hand, lifted it to his lips, and kissed the ring on the third finger of her left hand. "My mama gave me her wedding ring on my sixteenth birthday. I wore it on my pinkie ever since. Never knew I'd use it for a wedding ring for my bride, my beautiful star."

Laughing, she slapped his hand away. "Cut it out, Goldie. You're such a romantic!"

He took a deep breath. "I reckon you're right, but I love that you are here with me." He jumped up and glanced at his watch. "It's almost time for me to cut that record." He headed for the bathroom. "I gotta take a shower. Over his shoulder, he called out. "Get dressed and come with me." He tossed her the last biscuit from the brown paper bag. "Sorry, this'll have to do for breakfast."

One hour later, Goldie and El drove over to Phil's Studio on Beale Street, a place famous for letting both white and black people record. Goldie bragged about going to such a well-known location. "Mr. Tunstall, the agent here, said he wanted the best for me. Said it took a fat chunk of money to pay for the recording time. But he thinks I'm worth it. You married a man that's hot stuff, darlin'." He guffawed. "A sho 'nuff blues singer!"

After Sam Phil, the recording engineer, checked the equipment, Goldie got the signal to begin, and, with a pronounced black dialect, he sang into the mike as he strummed his guitar:

I got a feelin'

It got me reelin'

There is some news,

In this here blues.

I got a feelin'

Oh, got a feelin'

I'm tellin' you, here is some truth.

Look for the clues,

Here in the blues.

I got a feelin'

It got me reelin'

There's wrong and right,

And black and white.

I got a feelin'

It got me reelin'

There lies the cause

That I'll pay the cost.

I got a feelin'

Oh, got a feelin'.

You'll find the truth

Here in the blues.

Woman and man

There is a plan.

I got a feelin'

It got me reelin'

It won't be long
Before I'm gone.
I got a feelin'
Oh, got a feelin'

You'll find the truth
Here in the blues.
I got a feelin'
It got me reelin'

Eventually
Levees' floods redeem me.
I got a feelin'
It got me reelin'

Let justice come
For this wronged son.
I got a feelin'
Oh, got a feelin'

I'm tellin' you

Right here's the clues.

I got a feelin'

It got me reelin'.

El roamed around the studio while Goldie repeated the song five times to get the best recording. Mr. Phil kept adjusting the knobs, dials, and meters on his sound board until Mr. Tunstall nodded his head, satisfied.

They came out smiling and El grinned as Mr. Tunstall slipped a much-needed hundred-dollar bill to Goldie. "Here's a little to tide you over. Hope this record will be an instant hit. If it ain't, well, jes be patient. Keep on singing wherever you can git a gig." He placed both hands on his hips. "I got a big surprise for the two of you. Tomorrow morning, you've got an appointment to git some pictures made at Dutton's Studio. We'll need 'em for publicity." He put an arm around El. "And I'm gonna have one made of you and the groom as a wedding present. The photographer will put a rush on them; you can see proofs the next day and he'll make the prints right away." With a bow, he added, "One more thing. I made a couple of appointments for you to audition at some o' the most popular juke joints around Memphis."

Goldie reeled backward. "Wow!" Then his brow wrinkled. "But I can't afford to stay in *this* hotel." He pulled on his shirt. "I planned to wear my Zoot suit, my signature outfit, to those auditions. Hell, I don't have any other clothes with me and…"

Raising a palm, Tunstall stopped him. "Nothing to worry about; I'm taking care of all your expenses for the next few weeks." He handed El two twenty-dollar bills. "Get what you can with this. When we're not busy," he winked, "you and the missus can have time to have fun all alone."

The next day, the trio arrived at the photography studio and had shots made from every angle, with Goldie holding his guitar, and one of the two lovebirds. The photographer, a lively man and quick to laugh, even supplied a bouquet for El. She refused the veil he offered saying it wouldn't fit with the blue dress she'd bought that morning.

Two days later, when they got the finished black and white prints, Goldie said, "These are great. They make me look good." He grinned at El. "You don't need anything to make you look good. You're beautiful." Out of hearing of the photographer who was in the camera room with another customer, he pointed to a pose where he had a broad grin. "Now look at that. You can't see that it's gold, but my tooth sure is shining. I worked hard at the Mobile docks to get it when I was just sixteen. Cost almost a month's salary. First time I passed as white. Humph, I fooled that dentist." He wrinkled his brow. "He kept making slurs about black folks, though, and had me squirming in the chair. I reckon he thought I was just nervous." He stuck the photos back in a manila envelope. "Ha, won't Dr. Murphy be surprised if I get famous and he finds out he worked on a black man?"

He didn't dwell on the history of his gold tooth. They had other business to take care of, like clothing. Goldie called Wylie asking him to pack up some of his clothes and then give Mama Tippi a message to sneak out some of El's clothes, and mail them to him, promising to pay Wylie back for the postage. A follow up call from Wylie at the hotel front desk brought bad news. He could send Goldie's clothes but Mama Tippi said "I couldn't get none from El's room. Miss Elma she watch me too close." So El rotated wearing the red rose dress with the blue one every other day.

For the next two weeks, Tunstall, Goldie, and El made the rounds of juke joints around Memphis, setting up gigs. Four of the owners made offers right away after hearing Goldie sing and he was elated at the opportunities to launch his songs. In addition, the record was being played on local radio stations and getting good response. They were having a great time. Then Wylie called saying he needed his car back. To give Goldie time to get to Cleveland, pack his things, and perhaps find a way to get some of El's clothes—even if he'd have to steal them—he was scheduled to start playing at the juke joints in late November.

When Goldie and El shook hands with Tunstall before leaving Memphis, Tunstall handed Goldie two copies of the record he'd cut and two to El, along with giving both a business card. "Take care o' those records." He turned to Goldie. "Got some news for ya, Boy. My contacts at the biggest radio station in Memphis are payin' off. I'm goin' ovah there with yo record. They agreed to a contract; they love it."

"You kiddin' me, Mr. Tunstall?"

"Nope." He patted his jacket. "Told 'em I got you under contract." He grinned at El. "If somethin' happens to Goldie, yo names on here. You could be fixed for life." He gave a guffaw. But Goldie's young and healthy; not much chance o' that." He kissed El's cheek. "Young lady, you take good care o' this guy. I got faith in him. He sings and his git-tar answers." He shook his finger at Goldie. "This boy's got soul. And some kinda style nobody else has touched on. With you by his side, he's gonna be a star someday. Maybe soon. Jes you watch and see."

Before Goldie left town, he and El had lunch bypassing the "White's Only" sign on the diner down the street. His Creole heritage served him well. Nobody questioned Goldie's passing as white or refused to serve them hamburgers and French fries. Goldie chatted to El about the record and all the contacts Mr. Tunstall had. Tightening his grip on his wife's hand, he promised, "Baby, I ain't got much now, but I got a feelin' in my bones that God's shining his light, his star, down on me. He's gonna bless my singing and one day, I'll buy you the moon. Or whatever you ask for." He leaned forward, kissed her behind her ear, and whispered, "I love you."

El smiled, she was determined to stay encouraging. Her thoughts drifted, not to the future, but to the present. She waved at Goldie as he pulled out of the parking lot, his red hair blowing in the wind, and he waved his hat through the air. "I love you, El Parsons," he yelled as he headed towards Mississippi, "I will love you to the day I die!"

She watched as he disappeared down the highway, tears running down her face as she walked back to the hotel. She wondered how she would survive the next week; she had never been alone away from home before. The plan was for her to stay at the hotel until Goldie went back to Cleveland and returned by Greyhound to Memphis. But could he get more gigs when he came back? What if they couldn't afford to stay in the hotel? Tunstall couldn't keep paying their way for long. Where would they live; how would they eat? Those questions had no answers. *Love must be blind. What in the world have I gotten myself into?*

Chapter 7

Fearful that she'd miss his call, El spent the afternoon sitting in a straight-backed, wooden chair in the hotel lobby reading advice columns in year-old magazines. One bit of guidance to the lovelorn caught her interest. It wasn't about the problems in a black and white marriage, but one dealing with a white girl marrying a Hispanic. That young couple had also left their small hometown in Clio, Alabama, and moved to Memphis. El could tell by the letter how deeply people in Barbour County, Alabama frowned on such a marriage. The response was not objective. Prejudice was evident in every line. The advisor, Miss Helen Helpful, wrote, "Now what did you expect? Since you were raised in Alabama, it would seem that following the long-standing culture of your parents, neighbors, and friends would have rubbed off on you. Perhaps you might consider moving North to a more tolerant area if you intend to continue to "break the rules." However, you may find reactions there, or anywhere else, not to your liking." It concluded, "Sorry, I can't be more sympathetic."

El fumed as she tossed the magazine aside. *Will people ever change? Oh, Goldie, I love you so. I can handle others objecting, but I'm Mamma's only child. Doesn't she want me to be happy? Why does she refuse to accept that we want to be together?*

The phone on the reception clerk's desk jingled and he called out, "Mrs. Parsons, here's the long-distance call you've been waiting for."

Jumping up, El darted for the desk. When she picked up the phone and heard Goldie's voice, she sighed. "Oh, sweetheart, I'm so glad to hear your voice. I thought you'd call last night. I was worried."

"El, you won't believe what's going on here. I'm in a phone booth next to the Market and I only have a few nickels and dimes, but I'll try to sum up what is going on. I was gettin' my stuff from Wylie's and along comes Eli Tarsi. Since we left, Wylie told me he has been hanging around, showing off and gossiping about everything, and writing in the little notebook you told me about. It is creepy. He spends a lot of time in the sheriff's office; they pay him to clean it up once a week. It's the only time we can do anything without him hovering about. One day we managed to get with Mr. Tunstall and...that's too long a story. I'll tell you more about that later.

"When Eli saw me, he asked about you! Then he rattled on about your mamma and how he'd do anything for her. Him and his 'Mama says to do whatever Mrs. Elma tells me.' Then he talks about how Mrs. Elma's putting on airs. He's right. Boy, is your mamma a piece of work! She's telling everybody you ran off with a lawyer, a white guy almost twice your age. I think Eli's a little jealous of you."

"What?" El screeched out.

The phone crackled, but El could make out, "I planned to take the bus, but Wylie said he's gotta make a trip to Memphis in a few days, so I can hitch a ride with him. There's more to Eli's story, so I'll write you a letter with all the sorry details. Too many people close by to tell you on the phone. It ain't good, El. Darn it, here comes Eli. Got to go! Love you! Bye."

He hung up the phone with a click. El didn't get a chance to ask more questions, but her brain whirled. As she ascended the rickety stairs, she formed a mental picture of Eli Tarsi, a squatty little guy who lived on the outskirts of Cleveland with his mother. Though kinky-haired, he was white but always had a heavy tan from doing odd jobs for plantation owners or anyone else who'd hire him. He'd strut up with his slew-footed walk acting as if he owned any property he was on. Right in a person's face, he'd start by saying, "I need a job; I'm taking care of my mother." Then he'd rant on, spitting all over people as he spoke. Any subject brought up, he'd claim to know all about.

One thought made El smile. Eli was a lapsed Catholic who hadn't seen the inside of Our Lady of Victories Church in many years, much to his mother's dismay. Didn't stop him from using it to help him get out of trouble. Elma didn't seem to notice how ironic that was.

Since Eli worked cheap, Elma hired him. Then she'd brag to her society friends, "I don't mind helping Eli. He's about forty now and not quite right, but he does help his mother. I'm blessed. It's my Christian duty to help those less fortunate."

But El felt her mamma had a couple of other motives for tolerating the obnoxious bore. Eli brought her all the latest gossip. He also spread the word about how Elma Tollar contributed to charitable causes and to society in Cleveland. He made Elma look good and she loved it. He was doing that now by circulating the rumor that Eleanor "had married well." Plus, he was in so much awe of the rich female plantation owner that he'd do anything in the world she asked, anything. Besides, that's what his momma told him to do.

El unlocked the door to her hotel room and plopped on the bed. *How long will it take for Goldie's letter to get here? What else is going on? Goldie said it isn't good. I don't like that. Mamma sure made up a tall tale this time, but she always does whatever it takes to make herself look good. She's sure mad I didn't go through with making my debut and end up marrying someone with position and money."*

In a fit of frustration, El jumped off the bed, stormed into the bathroom and stared into the mirror. Her brown eyes set in an oval face stared back at her. She stepped closer, letting her hundred and fifteen-pound frame lean against the lavatory at the hip line. She spoke aloud: *Listen, Eleanor Tollar, I mean Parsons, you're a married woman now. Act like one, even if you're still seventeen years old.*

Marching into the bedroom, she looked towards the bed and the wrinkled pile of covers where Goldie had slept. *Oh, Goldie, please hurry back. I need you and you've got me worried. I hope that letter comes soon so I can find out what the problem is. I pray you're just overreacting.* She chewed on her lower lip, drawing a trickle of blood. After wiping it off with her fingers, she glanced at them. *Geez, I bet Eli's already told Mamma Goldie's in Cleveland. No tellin' what she'll do.* She cut her eyes upward. *Oh, Daddy, you could always keep Mamma under control. I need you. How I wish you were here.*

But he wasn't. Neither was her husband. She pulled down the window shade but didn't turn on the ceiling light in the center of the room. Standing there in the dark trapped in circumstances over which she had no control, she felt more alone than she ever had before. The words of Jesus on the cross "My God, my God, why have you forsaken me?" kept floating through her mind. She dropped back onto the bed, pulled the covers over her head, and sobbed into her pillow.

Chapter 8

Two days later, El took the letter addressed to her from the hotel desk clerk with shaky hands. Glancing at Goldie's sprawling handwriting where he'd written, "Mrs. Eleanor Parsons," she grinned as she stuffed the envelope in the pocket of her dress. Then she returned to the room she'd hibernated in since he left. She'd wanted to go to Beale Street, but not alone.

El sat on the corner of the bed, muscles tense as she tore open the side of the envelope, and pulled out the letter. Unfolding it, seeing where the black ink bled between the blue lines, she prayed, *Dear God, please don't let this be too bad.* She read her husband's words:

MY Wife,

I miss you already. but Wylie says we'll leave for Memphis the day after tomorrow. We had a little fuss the other day at the Crossroads near your mamma's house. I think he's jealous of me about my record. Plus, he wants me to kind of go into business with him. You know, cut records together. He'd have me focus on that, not my marriage. I'm not ready to sell my soul to the devil for fame and money. I wouldn't agree with him, he's still gonna give me a ride to Memphis. I promise you we will be back together soon. I want to get out of Cleveland as fast as I can. Your mamma knows I'm here. Big mouth Eli spilled the beans. Damn him. Oh, I ain't scared of her. Don't you worry. I don't want no trouble. I'll just stay out of her way. But I had to come to town to mail this letter so it'd get to you quick. I guess maybe I overreacted after talking with Cheche. That little girl is full of the mojo and she told me to be wary of floods and some other stuff. Somehow she had me all tied up with Mama Tippi and doing anything for fame and money. Don't mean nothing though, I guess. Kinda scared me, sometimes I get vibes about what's going to happen. But you don't believe all that stuff, so you're okay. I'm worried about one thing. You know, a white man is idealized if he rebels against injustice and fights the system. A black man is not. They expect us to be loyal and humble and never complain, just to accept any orders they give us. If you're in the skin of a white man, anything you say about justice or against the system makes you a hero; but if you're in the skin of a black man, the same words are considered impudent and unnatural. Yeah, they'll sure say our marriage is unnatural. We're supposed to keep our place. But that don't change nothing far as I'm concerned. I just had to tell you how I feel; I can't say any more.

Here's all my hugs and kisses and love,

YOUR husband, Goldie

El made two fists, crumbling the letter, but then pressed it into the bed to try and smooth it back out. *What in the world does that last paragraph really mean? Is Goldie being threatened by someone? The language is a little philosophical for him. Sounds like Mamma telling him to "Keep his place." Plus that, I bet he's just reacting to Cheche's mojo predictions.* She thought of the words in the song, "Eventually - Levees' floods redeem me," and smiled. The first letters of those two lines spelled his nickname for her, El. Then things turned dark again as the line, "Levees' floods redeem me," made her wonder how they tied in with Cheche's formidable forecasts. She shook her head to clear it. *No, no! I refuse to dwell on that. I don't believe in the mojo.*

She read the letter again, turning to other parts of Goldie's words. She didn't like her mamma or Che making her husband afraid. She wasn't worried much about her mamma bothering Goldie. No, to do that, she'd have to take back her lies that her daughter married a rich man. Besides, if El let it get out Elma was drinking and running around, her place in society would vanish. She clicked her tongue. She could also slough off Cheche's mojo ramblings, and Eli didn't have enough sense to cause any real trouble. But she wondered about the disagreement between Wylie and Goldie. Wylie had always been the big man in town. Was he afraid Goldie would take his place? What would he do about it?

Folding her arms, El shook her head. *Nothing. That's what Wylie would do. I'm just making something out of nothing. I have too much time to think. Cabin fever's getting its grip on me. I need to get out of this room. I may just go down to Beale Street and wander around. It's daylight. What am I afraid of anyhow?* But when she reached for the dress shop bag she had used for a purse, she remembered that it did not have her identification. It held the two records, her wedding license, and a copy of the contract with Tunstall with her signature, not a driver's license. So, she reconsidered. *I better just stay put. Goldie's bound to get here today or tomorrow.* She untied her shoestrings, pulled off her saddle shoes and white socks and stuffed the socks into the shoes. Aloud, she prayed, *Dear God, please send Goldie back to me. I need him.*

Chapter 9

El did not sleep well that night and did not awaken until the morning sun shined against the curtains. As soon as she heard the knock on her door, as she glanced at the clock, she woke up with a start. It was nine a.m. A second hard rap got her attention.

"Just a minute," she called out as she scurried out of the bed still wearing her underwear. In the bathroom, she slipped on her dress and looked in the mirror, smoothing her hair. "Almost ready!" she yelled towards the door.

El cracked open the door and gasped. "Wylie, I am so glad to see you!" She unhitched the slide lock and pulled open the door. She craned her neck to look past Wylie, thinking Goldie must be in the hall. She did not see him anywhere. Confused, she looked back at Wylie, "Where's Goldie? Isn't he with you?"

Wylie shook his head as he looked down, shifting one of the satchels he held on his shoulder, adjusting the strap so it didn't slip off. "Er, no, Miss El. Can I come in? I got a long story to tell you."

El poked out her bottom lip. *What to do? Should I let this black man in my room?* She had to. Maybe he was the only one who knew where Goldie was.

As if reading her mind and understanding her hesitation, Wylie reassured her. "Look, I ain't aimin' to do you no harm. It might look funny to see us together in the hotel lobby. Hell, I had to sneak up the stairs to get here. I wuz afraid somebody'd try to stop me in a white hotel."

She stared at his light skin.

"Oh, yeah, I've passed a few times." He leaned against the door frame. "But it don't always work. And I don't like doin' that."

El motioned, stepped aside, and walked behind him into the room. She had to find out about her husband. Wylie sat in the only chair in the room and she sat on the corner of the rumpled bed. "All right, Wylie," her whole body tensed, "tell me what's going on."

"I'm sorry, but you gotta know, Goldie's missin'. We had a, uh, talk the day before yesterday when I tole him I didn't like the idea o' him passin' as white and marrying outa his race."

El's mouth fell open, he knew her daddy and she regarded him as a friend, why did he betray her and Goldie?

Wylie shook his head. "Oh, no, Miss El. It ain't you. Well, it's dangerous for blacks marryin' whites. You may not realize this but some black folks won't like it none, either." He shook his head. "No sir, not a'tall. That mixin' up, kinda goin' to the other side, could ruin his career." Cocking his head, he added, "Since I'm his best friend and I been promoting him, it won't help mine none, either. We'd planned to cut records together, but well... Anyhow he stormed off and I ain't seen him since. Spent one whole day runnin' all ovah Cleveland askin' everbody if they seen him. No luck." He didn't give El a chance to interrupt but rattled on. "I waited as long as I could, but I hadda be here in Memphis today."

El's eyes became moist as she stammered out, "Where can he be? Why wouldn't he come back to me like he promised?" Wylie reached for her hand.

She snatched it away with a reflex action. How dare a black man be so audacious! Then her mouth fell open. *Oh, my God! I'm married to a black man.* "Wylie, I'm sorry. I..."

Wylie stood and nodded twice. "I'm sorry, too, Miss El. I know betta. I didn't mean to get personal with you and I shoulda stopped this before it started. No good'll come from mixin' and this be the proof." He gave a quick bow, and then handed her one of the worn leather satchels. "Here's Goldie's things, a suit, a pair of pants, some underwear, extra guitar picks, and some sheet music he neva used 'cause he wrote mosta his own songs. He musta been wearin' his purple Zoot suit and them fancy wing-tip shoes he loved." His Adam's apple bounced up and down as he turned before heading for the door. "He always took his guitar with him. He gave me a record he made but it got broke. Look, I'm real sorry. If I hear anything from Goldie, I'll get in touch with you. I promise."

"Wylie," she said as he turned to walk out the door, "Something good is going to come of this. I love Goldie and he loves me. We will work it out."

"Mrs. Parsons," he said as he turned to look into her eyes, "it's the blues, it never works out, that's why it is called the blues." Wylie tipped his hat and walked away.

El locked the door behind Wylie, but she couldn't lock out her problems. She lay face down on her pillow and flooded it with tears. Lifting her head, she sat up straight and sobbed, "Goldie, Goldie, where did you go? Promises, promises. You promised me we'd be back together soon. You even promised me the moon." Shaking her fist, she screamed to the faded papered walls, "I don't need the moon, but I do need you. You're my light and my star, too. I can't live without you. Come back, my darling, the love of my life, please come back."

But unlike the interaction in the blues songs Goldie sang, it wasn't call and response. The walls didn't answer.

Chapter 10

A few hours later, El stopped crying and forced herself to settle down. She had to make a plan. Wallowing in self pity wasn't going to bring Goldie back. But what to do? Who to consult? *Call Mamma? No, she wouldn't be any help; she'd be a hindrance.* Mama Tippi came to mind, but she had no phone. Besides, her daughter Cheche would be there too. But what about the mojo and her predictions, could they be true? Did the words in Goldie's song *Reelin' Feelin'* mean he had the "knowin' of what was comin'?" Distressed and confused, El doubted and questioned her own beliefs.

However, Tunstall had phoned her saying he was pleased that the record was doing well so fast. He hadn't seemed concerned about Goldie. He just said, "He'll show up." It made her think she shouldn't worry either. In a few minutes she shrugged off her negativity, refusing to believe anything bad had happened to her new husband.

El finally faced the fact that she had to get off her butt and start making adult decisions. She picked up Goldie's satchel and rummaged through the items in it. Wylie was right about the contents. No Zoot suit; he must

89

have been wearing it. She found a purple colored Bakelite button in a side pocket. It was one he'd asked her to sew back on his Zoot suit. Wondering if she'd ever get the chance to do that now, she put it back along with the wedding license, the record contract, the record she got from Turnstall, and the few dollars she had left. She stuffed her other dress inside, and closed the bag.

She had wasted the day crying over this mess and it was eight p.m. but she had to leave now. She had to find Goldie and time was of the essence when someone is missing. She couldn't wait till morning. She slung his satchel over her shoulder and made it down the steps to the front desk. "I'm leaving," she told the night clerk as she laid the room keys on the check-in desk. "Mr. Tunstall will pay the bill." After he nodded, she asked, "How do I get to the Greyhound station?"

"It's down the street on the right, just three blocks away." He frowned. "Where are you going, Miss? Not many buses leave at this time of night."

Adjusting the bag on her shoulder, she replied, "I'm going to Cleveland, MS."

"Oh," he said, "you're in luck. If you hurry, you can catch the last one headed south. It leaves at nine."

With that information, El rushed out the door, not yet deciding what she would do when she got back to her hometown. She hoped she could come up with something on the five hour bus ride, but she had little confidence about finding a solution.

She purchased her ticket, happy that it was cheap and she had money left. The bus arrived on time, but it wasn't full. El took a seat three rows back from the driver. The bus would make several stops and if she wanted to get off, sitting up front was convenient. Using the satchel as a pillow, she wiggled into a comfortable position, and closed her eyes hoping to get some sleep. As they roared down the highway, however, she couldn't force her problems off her mind.

First, I'll have to find a place to stay. Mama Tippi practically raised me; she'll put me up for a while. I can trust her not to tell anyone I'm in town. But how can I hunt for Goldie? Well, in Cleveland, he'd stay in the row houses at another plantation in town. He wouldn't stay at Tollar. . But I want the sheriff's help. I'll have to tell him Goldie's missing. She tapped her lip. *This isn't going to work. I can't keep my presence a secret. No. I'll need to openly look for Goldie myself. That sheriff's not going to look too hard for a black man, not even for me, a Tollar. Mamma will stop him too. Searching for Goldie won't be on the top of his list. After a few days, he'll give it up. If anybody finds Goldie, it'll have to be me.*

El took a deep breath as other problems surfaced. *How am I going to survive on the little money I have left?* She fingered the bills in her pocket. *These won't last long. Mamma hardly let me out of her sight, so I don't have any friends to borrow money from, or relatives either. Oh, Daddy, if only you were still alive. You'd help me.* Then she said aloud, "Wouldn't you?"

The bus driver turned his head. "You talking to me, Miss?"

"Never mind," she replied at the realization she'd blurted out her words.

He nodded and concentrated on driving. El's thoughts reverted to her problems and a partial solution. *Mamma will be gone to her bridge club meeting tomorrow. Maybe I can sneak in the house and get some clothes and my purse.* Her eyes popped wide open. *Ah, ha. I can also get that diamond ring that's supposed to be my graduation present. Hmm, Mamma doesn't know I found it hidden in an ice cube in a tray in the refrigerator. She never thought I'd find it in the little freezer part. It's a family heirloom worth at least two thousand dollars. I can sell it. Humph! Fat chance. Nobody I know has that kind of money to buy it. Who does? Hmm, I heard the stories about how they pawned it during hard times to save the farm and later bought it back. They joked about how no questions were asked in Meridian. I can pawn it there.*

With a resolution to one of her problems figured out, El managed to turn off her brain. She leaned back and fell asleep, dreaming of sewing that button on Goldie's Zoot suit while he watched. The bus made the normal stops and picked up a few more passengers, others reached their destinations and left, but El didn't get off. She stirred when people passed by but kept her eyes shut. She had to be as rested as possible when she arrived in Cleveland in order to face her ordeal.

At two a.m. the Cleveland, MS, Greyhound Station was all but deserted. While she dozed on the bus, rain clouds moved into the area, drenching everything. The awning in front of the bus station had a few bums hunkered down underneath, filling the uncomfortable seats. This night, the station night guard had let them stay. He usually ran them off, but he wasn't so cruel that he'd send those down on their luck men into the pouring rain. El felt sorry for the men, but she didn't offer any help as she normally would have. She had to find Goldie. A loud crackle from the sky flashing with lightning and a new intensity to the rain caused her to pause. Good sense outweighed desperation and she decided to wait out the storm in the Greyhound bus' waiting room.

Two hours later the rain lightened up but did not stop. It was almost four a.m. El was dozing on the hard slatted seats in the bus station when a short man walked into the room. She recognized him instantly and asked, "Eli, what in the world are you doing here so early?" It was really a rhetorical question. Eli had a habit of hanging out at the bus station. He knew some of the clerks who tolerated him. He'd pick up a little money driving people home, especially late at night. But her curiosity stirred and she wondered, *Did someone tell Eli I was here?*

With a hand on his hip, he looked straight at her. "Well, Miss Eleanor, I could ask you the same question, but I know it ain't my business, is it? I reckon you've come to check on your mamma. She sure ain't doing good after that stroke. Can't talk or speak..."

"Stroke! My God!" She reeled backward. "When did Mamma have a stroke? What happened?"

"Miss El," he said in a raspy voice, "you mean you didn't know? It happened about a week after you ran off with your rich man. Before that, she'd already had a sprained ankle from that tussle with you." He glared at her and then raised his voice, making sure people around him could hear. "You think about that. A good daughter would check on their mamma. Not you. So, you're too good for us now."

El's lips made a straight line and her face flushed red. "Where is Mamma?" She clenched her fists. *This changes everything. What to do?*

"She's at home. But she's not talkin' or nuthin'." He pulled a small notebook from his pant's pocket and jotted words on it.

El took a deep breath as she noticed the rain picking back up. Then she shook her head. She didn't want Eli's help, but he could provide her the quickest route to the house. "Take me to her." *Not much choice. She must be in a coma. No matter what, she is my mamma.*

Eli drove his rickety old blue Ford truck as close as he could to the station and she darted towards the passenger door, pulled it open and hopped in, belongings in hand. She scooted as far from Eli as she could as thoughts swirled around in her brain all the way home. Eli didn't seem to notice and rattled on about how her mamma was happy that she married well, but he fired a few pointed questions, "Did you really get married to a rich lawyer up there in Memphis, Miss Eleanor? What's your new name?"

When El ignored him and continued to stare at the streaks of rain dancing on the windshield as they raced down the road, he mumbled, "We all know Miss Elma don't mind stretching the truth. Best not to pay too much attention to what she says, if she ever can say anything again."

It seemed like an hour, but the trip only took ten minutes. When they arrived at her house, El tossed her last few dollars on the car seat and Eli flew away in the truck. She dashed up the front steps and her head spun from a flashback of her mamma knocking her down there, reminding her of their last encounter. Could she forgive that and handle this? It was a horrible turn of events. The only upside was that now she could stay in her own room on the Tollar Plantation. She did take comfort in that realization.

She hurried into her mamma's bedroom in the back of the house and saw Mama Tippi sitting in a rocking chair. It was a stark reminder of the same scene she shared with her daddy a year ago. Only this time, it was her mother in the four poster bed, pale skinned and close to death. It was only a matter of time before she too would be gone forever.

Mama Tippi nodded at her. El saw the worry in her eyes. "Cheche said you'd be here, and she spoke the truth. I'm glad you are." She shook her head and then leaned over to brush back a lock of Elma's hair. "Miss Elma done been like this a week or so. I cain't do much fo' her, but I stays at night and keeps her company She done got bad off, Miss Eleanor. She cain't talk o' nuthin."

Tears ran down El's cheeks as she sat on the edge of the bed and took her mamma's limp hand into her own, noticing how the bright blue veins shone through her pale skin. "Mamma," she whispered. "It's Eleanor. Can you hear me?" This was not how things should be. The sadness of it all made her heart ache. No winners in this affair.

Elma didn't stir. So El leaned closer to her mother's tightly shut eyes. "Try to open your eyes, Mamma, so you can see me." El's tears dropped on Elma's face, but not a muscle of the ill woman sturred.

El swallowed hard in an effort to control her sobbing. She glanced towards the reliable Mama Tippi and figured it was a safe bet the woman had talked to her daughter with the mojo. Cheche would've told her mom El had run off with Goldie, so she had no need to conceal that.

El squeezed Elma's hand, and said in a cracked voice, "I'm, I'm sorry, Mamma. I didn't mean to hurt you, but I had to go. I love Goldie. I had to be with him." She grinned as she held up her hand, flashing the ring on her finger. "We got married. I know you don't approve, but please try to understand. Now," she sobbed aloud, "now Goldie's missing and I can't find him." She leaned into the chair Mama Tippi pulled closer to the bed for her. "And you're sick and in a coma, and Daddy's gone. I don't have anybody." Tears flowed onto her cheeks.

Mama Tippi stood and put her arm around El's shoulder. "She cain't hear you, Miss Eleanor. I know you'se tired. Cheche, she say you got otha troubles. Why don' you go ta bed and we'll talk 'bout this tomorrow mornin'?"

El stiffened. "I'll be alright. This is such a shock." She bit the corner of her lip.

El wasn't sure she'd feel safe alone anywhere, even in her own bedroom, but she didn't admit it. She picked up her few belongings, kissed her mother's cheek, hugged Mama Tippi, and left the room.

El walked down the hall towards the stairs and her room as it brightened with the rising sun, but she chose not to go to bed. Instead, she went outside through the front door, took the porch steps two at a time, and walked aimlessly down the dirt road for about ten minutes, heading nowhere. The rain had subsided and the sun was rising over the cotton fields, but the events over the past twenty-four hours overwhelmed her. It matched the way her brain was functioning. All became strange; nothing was familiar. Who was she: Eleanor Tollar or El Parsons? She needed someone to make decisions for her badly. Her father was dead; he couldn't help. Her mother was dying; she wouldn't help anyway. She didn't have a husband; he was missing. She'd never felt so alone, so desolate. She made a couple of circles, then turned around. Where was she? Shocked, she stared at the Sunflower River, not far from where she sat with Goldie making plans for his music. Completely disoriented, El staggered around, her heart hurting, wondering if it was worth it to take the path back to the Tollar Plantation.

Chapter 11

After a short nap, when Eleanor opened her eyes, she had to orient herself to her surroundings. The bed was comfortable, the sheets were clean, and the breeze from the river flowed through her opened bedroom window. Events over the last few days flooded back--the planned search for Goldie, the bus ride, then the shock of Eli's revelation about her mother, now immobile and helpless. But her last memory was being outside as the sun rose. She had no memory of getting to her room and into bed. She lifted the covers and looked down to see she was still wearing her dress; one of two she had worn in the last few weeks. She hopped out of bed, disrobed, and got into a steamy, hot bathtub.

As she scrubbed off two days of grime with rose-scented soap, some of Eli's words popped into her brain. It hadn't registered before because she was so tired, but he'd called her "Miss El." Nobody called her that except Goldie. Eli never did before; he always said, "Miss Eleanor" when speaking to her. Then it lost importance. *Eli's odd. It's just a coincidence. I can't become suspicious of everything or let these superstitious things get to me or I'll go crazy. Mojo, kojo. So what? I've got to keep a clear head to deal with all these mind-boggling situations.* She took clean clothes out of her closet, grateful to be able to choose from more than two dresses, and braced herself as she went to her mamma's room. More new clothes were there. She tried not to tear up as she looked at the fluffy pink gowns her mother had chosen for her. *Things are so different now,* she thought as she headed down the stairs.

El walked into the room to see a small person leaning over the bed. On the tips of her toes she tried to spoon a little liquid down Elma's Throat. The cup of brown broth was sitting on the nightstand. As the person turned around to fill the spoon with more broth she looked up at El.

"Good evenin'," Cheche said. "How you doin', Miss Eleanor?" She pointed to the spoon in her hand. "Miss Elma, she can swallow, so I'm tryin' to get her to take a little o' this."

"How's Mamma doin', Cheche?"

Cheche looked at the floor. "She not good. Not good t'all." She raised her head and cast her big brown eyes to the ceiling. I warned her. I warned Goldie, and," she stared at El, "I warned you. What I said came true."

El cringed as she met Cheche's eyes and then looked away. When Cheche started her mojo, she often spoke in rhyme. She cast her eyes back at the girl and asked, "What do you mean, Cheche?"

"Nobody knows what I saw, if people don't listen, things come from afar." She added, "Grandma Dee's done gone away; more will happen any day."

El stepped close to Cheche's face, "I don't understand. Please tell me what you're talking about Cheche."

El's plea did no good. Cheche acted as if she didn't hear the question and resumed spooning liquid down Elma's throat. El shrugged and headed for the kitchen where Mama Tippi stood over the stove scrambling eggs. It was suppertime, but breakfast food was quick to fix, so they often prepared it when there was so much to do in the house.

"Afternoon, Miss Eleanor. You got a good rest?," Mama Tippi asked. "You must be hungry. Bet you ain't et since yesterday."

El didn't correct her bad grammar. "Mmm, smells wonderful. Can't wait to eat some of your biscuits. I did get some sleep and I am hungry, very hungry." She sat at the kitchen table.

Placing a plate with bacon, grits, a hot, buttered biscuit and the freshly cooked eggs in front of El, Mama Tippi ordered, "Now you eat all of that, y'hear?" She sized up El. "Yo got yo'self all skinny. Bet you lost mor'n ten pounds."

El chuckled, the first time she'd laughed since she'd been with Goldie. "Don't you worry about me. I'm fine." She swallowed some of the eggs. "But I'm confused. Mama Tippi, please tell me all about what happened. I also need to know what Cheche is ranting about; she's talking in rhyme like she does when she gets all wound up. I don't understand at all."

Mama Tippi nodded. While she washed dishes, she related what happened step by step. "Yo' mamma, she was all tore up and actin' mean when you left. Her mood changed when she told that story 'bout you marryin' a rich man, but we knew different. Mr. Wylie, he done tole us the truth." She turned and winked at Eleanor. "Cheche figured out first time she saw you look at Goldie you wuz in love. Didn't surprise us none when you ran off together." Mama Tippi let out her breath. "Some o' my folks didn't like no white gal marryin' up with our own, 'specially one we figure gonna be a famous blues singer one day. No, suh! We like to keep them fo' our own." She shrugged. "Not me, tho. I don't think that way. Two people in love oughta be togetha, no matta what! I believe in love." She clapped her hands three times.

"Okay, back to Mrs. Elma. After you left, she didn't come outa the house all day. News travels fast. Stories went round and round. Cheche kept saying: 'It's sad. Things gonna be bad, bad, bad.' And they were. First, tho, yo mamma thought up that story 'bout you marryin' a rich man. 'Course I knew betta, but I didn't pass it around; kep' it all to myself." She rubbed her chin. "We heard tell o' all kinda things, like somebody said they saw yo mamma talkin' to Wylie and to ol' gossipy Eli.. We figured she wuz makin' shore to spread the word of yo fine pick of a husband."

Mama Tippi halfway covered her mouth with both hands. "Then it came to a screechin' halt. Ol' Doc Barker said he got a phone call late one night from Mrs. Elma. She wuz slurrin' her words and beggin' for help. Well, he dashed right ovah to here and found her slumped down on the floor in the hallway." She shook her head. "Couldn't do much for her, so he called me and I came right over. He found a note by the phone in her handwriting. She'd wrote, "No hospital." We being doin' what little we can for her. Doc comes every day. He left some medicine but I don't' know what it is. I gives it to her like the directions say."

El felt as zapped as if she'd been plowing fields all day. She asked her surrogate mother's advice. "What can I do, Mama Tippi? I know Mamma. She always refused to go to a hospital, even when I was born."

"They can't do much for her anyhow, Miss Eleanor. I'd respect her wishes. When her time comes, she gonna go anyhow. You gotta accept God's will." She folded her hands and raised her eyes to heaven. "I do." Then she turned and gasped out. "Lord knows I had to with Grandma Dee. She gone. Cheche tell you that?"

"She did. What happened?"

"Oh, nobody knows. She disappeared. Nobody even saw her leave." She narrowed her eyes. "'Lessen Cheche did, but she won't tell."

El sighed at the talk of the mojo. That's what it was about even if the word wasn't used. No need to pursue it; Mama Tippi didn't know anything else and Cheche wasn't going to reveal one more word than she wanted to. Changing the subject, El switched to her reason for returning home in the first place, her search for Goldie.

After taking a bite of the biscuit, she said to Mama Tippi, "Do you know Goldie is missing? Tell me whatever you can about him. He left me in Memphis and returned to town. What did he do when he came back to Cleveland? Did you see him?"

Mama Tippi nodded as she picked up El's empty plate. "Yes, I saw him once. I was passin' by the Crossroads when he and Wylie wuz, well, they wuz fightin' but jes talkin' loud next to Wylie's car. I couldn't hear no words but they wuz both yellin'. I hung 'round long enuf to see Goldie snatch up his bag out of the backseat and head off, but I nevah saw nothin' else." She snapped her fingers. "They wuz one more thing. Looked like somebody wuz followin' Goldie, he wasn't very tall, maybe a kid, I couldn't tell for sure. They wuz too far away and my eyesight ain't too good nohow."

"Try to think, Mama Tippi. It's very important. Was it a boy, a man, or a girl? What kind of clothes did the person have on?" El had gotten to her feet and walked

104

next to Mama Tippi. She grabbed a towel to help dry the dishes.

Mama Tippi frowned as she passed El a wet plate. "Pants, yeah, pants. Mighta been a boy. I cain't be shore, tho."

It was a start. *Mamma has somebody to stay with her. I can't do anything anyway. After all, I came here to search for my husband.* It had been unusually warm this summer, but a refreshing cool breeze moved in during the day. El checked on her mother and then walked out the door when she saw Cheche sitting with her. El told her, "Cheche, I'll be back in a while, call Doctor Barker if you need help."

El picked the car keys out of her mamma's purse and walked down to the other side of the cotton bin where they kept the tractors. It was also where the Buick was kept. As she drove off in it and flew down the dirt road towards town, a thought drifted through her mind: *Who was following Goldie? Wylie? Or could it have been Eli? What happened if whoever it was caught up with my husband? Do I want to know? No, not if it's bad news. Regardless, I have to find out!*

First, El wanted to hear from the doctor, herself, about her mother's condition. She parked out front, walked to the door, and rang the bell at Dr. Barker's home office. After pulling the curtains aside and checking on the visitor, he opened the door.

"Miss Eleanor," he blurted out, "you're the last person I expected to see. Come in." The doctor sat in a well-worn leather chair behind his desk and motioned her to sit opposite him. "I guess you're here to ask about your mamma." He looked over horn-rimmed glasses perched on his nose. "I'm sorry but I can't give you any good news."

"Please tell me what happened."

Adjusting his signature bow tie, Doc said, "it was last Friday, November 28. Around midnight, my phone rang. At first, I couldn't tell who it was, then Elma blurted out her name. Then she started reeling off other names in an erratic order. Ha, in the middle of it, she said she needed help and ordered me to come to her house immediately."

El wrinkled her nose. "Whose names did she mention?"

"Yours, of course--three or four times. Then she said 'No black babies; paid Goldie; paid Eli all I promised him; don't owe anybody. I'll change my will; nothing for Eleanor after she disgraced me.' Of course, she couldn't speak clearly, but I managed to decipher what she said. She also told me not to send her to any hospital."

El took a deep breath. "I'm not surprised that she wanted to disown me, and I think I can understand why she mentioned Eli. He did work for her all the time and was always trying to get paid more than he was due, but I can't imagine why she said she paid Goldie."

"Oh, it's hard to make sense out of people in that condition, Eleanor. Don't worry about it." He got up and put his arm around her shoulder. "Be glad that your mamma didn't have a chance to change her will." He cleared his throat. "You're very young and you may have made a bad decision -- I heard about you and Goldie -- but you can change that with an annulment. Go back and finish high school and move on with your life." He pointed a finger at her. "Your daddy told me more than once his dream was for you to run the plantation one day. That's a golden opportunity for you." He leaned forward. "There's enough trouble in the world without adding personal problems to it, Eleanor. With the war in Europe escalating, our country may be in trouble soon and your generation will have to handle it." He pointed to a picture of Franklin Delano Roosevelt hanging on the wall behind him. "That man can't walk, but I am very much afraid he's going to have to take some big steps soon."

Eleanor rose and he escorted her to the door. "No need to feel guilty, Eleanor. What's done is done. You can't do anything for your mamma, except rectify your mistake, so go on with your life."

She didn't reply as he shut the door behind her. Gritting her teeth, she stomped away as fast as her legs would take her and got into the Buick. No need to ask the doctor about Goldie. He disapproved of the marriage and he wasn't on her side. If he knew anything, he wouldn't have told her. The tires squealed as she pressed hard on the gas, her next stop would be the sheriff's office on Main Street.

Husk Grimes had been Bolivar County's highest-ranking law enforcement official all of El's life. He'd stopped by for coffee every week when her daddy was alive to discuss the town's troubles and possible solutions. When she was a little girl, he'd pretend to pull a quarter from his ear and give it to her. He drove by often now to check things around the plantation. He liked hearing the music playing on the cotton bin porch, especially when they played Goldie's songs, but El didn't think Husk liked Elma. He acted politely when she was around and he tolerated her, like he considered doing so was his duty.

At almost three-hundred pounds, mostly muscle, Husk was a six-foot-three inch hulk of a man and no one messed with him. His build and his deep voice commanded respect. He also had a habit of raising up on and balancing on his toes which made him seem even more formidable. Today, though, when El entered, he was seated in his chair, behind his large wooden desk, and talking on the black rotary phone. He motioned her to come in and sit down as he balanced the receiver between his chin and shoulder. El chose a straight-backed chair across from his desk and sat on the soft cushion.

After reaching up to cover the mouthpiece with his hand, Husk whispered, "Be with you in just a moment," as he dug through the mound of papers on his desk with the other hand and pulled out an official looking piece of paper. "I have the proof right here in my hands," he said in a stern voice. "Bring that man in."

He hung up the phone, got up, walked around the desk, and bent over to give El a hug. "Long time since I've seen you, young lady. Heard you created quite a stir." He rested his hands on her shoulders and then held her back from him. "Well, you look mighty pretty. You break any laws? Here to turn yourself in?' He guffawed. "If I heard right, you might have broken one." He glanced down at her wedding ring, wrinkling his brow. "Times are changing, but not here yet. Just don't come to town together, you hear?"

"Sounds like you know about me and Goldie. Sheriff, we will leave Cleveland. We plan to go back to Memphis. We want no trouble, but I can't find him. After we got married in Memphis, he drove back to Cleveland to return Wylie Martin's car. He wrote me one letter, it was stamped from Cleveland, but he never came back to me. I can tell you how he was dressed; he had on his purple Zoot suit. You know, the one he wears when he's working a show."

El pulled out the purple colored button and showed it to the sheriff. "This is a button I needed to sew on Goldie's Zoot suit, but I never got the chance. It's the same color as the suit, if that helps. Anyhow, in Memphis, Goldie made a record and things were going fine. He had some gigs lined up there and we were going to stay away for good. Something's wrong; Goldie wouldn't leave me like this. He loved me. He would've come back to get me." Her voice broke. "I need to find him, Husk. Can you help me? Daddy's dead and Mamma's dying--she's against this and wouldn't help anyway. Since Goldie lived in the county, you're the only one I have to turn to."

Husk signed deeply as he rose to his toes and leaned in to look into her eyes. "Eleanor, it would've been illegal for you to get married here, so you went to Memphis. Not a good decision, but sometimes we do stupid things. Heard your mamma's fake stories, too. But this is the first time I heard of Goldie's being missing." He cocked his head. "Tell you what I will do. I'll check around and write up a report. You need to know how black men are, they have a reputation for leaving when problems come up. And this sure is a problem. Black and white is kinda like oil and water. They just don't mix in this town."

El glared at him, "Goldie's a human being. One I love. I'm convinced he didn't run off. Can't you do something?"

"Ah, girl. You're taking this too seriously. It's just puppy love. A crush. Maybe you're just upset over your Daddy dying and your mamma being sick." He patted her shoulder. "Let this go. Take care of your mamma and run that plantation like the folks in your family did before you." He opened the door for her, signaling their conversation was almost over, "I tell you what; if I find out anything, I'll let you know. I promise. I'll also start on the missing person's report."

Husk walked her to the door, but she knew when it slammed behind her there was no point in coming back. El felt desolate, but she wasn't going to give up. If nobody else would look for Goldie, she'd look for herself. No matter how long it took, she was going to find her husband and they were going to stay married, despite what the world said. Her war was on!

***

El's world consisted of spending the morning with her comatose mother, and helping Mama Tippi and Cheche feed and clean her up. They made sure her afternoons were free so she could drive all around nearby counties in her mamma's Monterey Blue Buick with a white top and whitewall tires. She ventured to the row house shacks at other plantations, to grocery stores, and at night she caused a ruckus when she pranced into juke joints. Many entertainers would not talk to her inside, so she'd wait for them by the backdoor after they played and sang. A couple of them told her they'd seen Goldie or maybe said "Hello," but that was about it. The most irritating thing for El was that nobody admitted seeing the argument between Goldie and Wylie.

As she got closer to her eighteenth birthday, December 7, 1941, she became increasingly concerned and frightened. The fear of being alone resulted in an impulsive moment. El left home, not telling anyone, at ten a.m., filled up the gas tank of her mamma's Buick, and headed for Memphis. She still had Tunstall's address and phone number. Mr. Tunstall might have Wylie's new number. It was a long shot, but it was the only thing she had not tried. Maybe one of them could tell her what happened to her husband.

She was almost to Clarksdale when she turned on the radio and fought to keep the car on the road as she was shocked by Goldie's song playing. It was the first time she had heard his voice in weeks and the tears began to flow. But his song was soon interrupted by a horrifying announcement--one she couldn't believe.

The broadcaster shared in a passionate voice that Pearl Harbor was under attack by the Japanese and American ships full of sailors were being sunk. Hawaii was under siege. She couldn't believe it. How could this happen to the United States of America? Her war took second place; another monumental war was now on. She couldn't continue her quest now. She turned the car around and drove straight back to Cleveland. When she arrived back home, Mama Tippi and Cheche acted as if she never left.

The next day, after a radio was moved into her mother's bedroom, Doc Barker's words haunted El when President Franklin Delano Roosevelt asked Congress to declare war saying, "Yesterday, December 7, a date which will live in infamy, the United States of America was suddenly and deliberately attacked by naval air forces of the Empire of Japan." Not only her world but everyone else's seemed to be falling apart. Still, there was nothing she could do but help take care of her mother. Elma was wasting away as her body struggled to breathe, but she still held onto life.

Just when El thought nothing worse could occur, more problems ensued. Two days later when her period was due, nothing happened. Nor did anything happen for the next week. Plus, Mamma was failing fast and by the middle of the week, she had another stroke. Doc Barker was called and talked with El by her bedside, "I know it's hard keeping her here, but let her have her wish. Don't put her in the hospital. Let her die at home, Eleanor, it will not be much longer."

During those remaining days, El didn't leave the house. Mama Tippi took care of everything so that El could sit by her bed. El knew she needed to forgive her mother, but her heart wasn't in it. The doctor had spread the word that these were Elma's last days. People came by to pay their last respects; the sheriff, Elma's bridge group, and a few neighbors.

Finally, Eli came by claiming he wanted to finish a job painting the front porch but El didn't want to be bothered. He didn't like that. "Your mamma owes me more for what I did," he said. "You better pay me. They'll be trouble if you don't, Miss El-eanor. Trouble with something you don't know nothing about. I fixed lotsa things."

To get rid of Eli, she gave him two twenty dollar bills she pulled out of her mother's purse. "Now don't come back, Eli," she said firmly. "This is it. This is my place now and you are not needed here ever again."

Eli stomped away mumbling, "You'll be sorry. This isn't the end of things. Wait and see." She saw him stop under a tree by the drive leading away from the house, pull out his pencil and write in the small notebook. She returned to the house to check on her mother. *I don't have time for crazy.*

Thirty minutes later, El was back on the porch rocking in her father's favorite chair. Mamma was near death. Her breathing had been strained all day. Mama Tippi came out and tapped her on the shoulder. "Miss Eleanor, it's time," she said. El went inside and sat by her mamma until she took her last breath. She wanted to feel grief, sorry to see her go, and she did in a way. Still, her emotions were mixed.

The next few days were a blur as funeral arrangements were made and papers were signed. The Tollar name drew a crowd at the funeral. The Baptist minister had written a glowing word picture of Elma's life and good deeds for the local newspaper since El couldn't bring herself to do it. After the funeral, people offered sympathy and condolences as they brought sweet tea, pimento cheese sandwiches, and a variety of salad and desserts for the crowd that filled the house, but to El it was as if she were living in a dream. She did the things she was supposed to do, accepting condolences, receiving hugs, but in reality she was disconnected from it all. To make things worse, the food made El sick to her stomach.

No matter how she felt, nothing was going to stop her. That night she managed to pack with plans to leave Cleveland forever the next morning. She crammed her suitcase with clothes from her closet, and looked for a bag for her shoes.

In her parent's room, she spotted an old rucksack in the corner of her mother's chiffarobe. She remembered it was where her father usually kept his Colt .38 revolver. When she opened it, she expected to see the gun; instead, it held some old clothes of her daddy's. El was so tired of this craziness; her mamma must have sold the pistol along with father's watch and wedding ring.

Her mamma wasn't sentimental, so El wasn't surprised, but she was surprised to find, at the bottom of the sack, a package of bullets along with a sales slip. However, when she couldn't make out the date of purchase, she put both back in the chiffarobe and moved on.

Back in her own room, she glanced at her Mamma's will, one she'd just gotten yesterday from the lawyer's office. Elma hadn't had time to change it. Everything was left to El--the plantation, the land, and the house. Despite the twinge of guilt that she couldn't fulfill her daddy's dream, it didn't matter to her any longer. She didn't want any more to do with the house or those prejudiced people. She rested her hand on her stomach that was still flat and decided she didn't want to raise a child in such a hostile environment. Worse yet, from all indications things weren't going to change anytime soon.

Exhausted, she tossed the will on the bedside table and curled up in her bed for one last time. She tried to sleep, but couldn't; the war, and her own private war in the community, kept her tossing and turning. When she dozed and her dreams focused on Goldie, she broke into a sweat. Why wasn't he with her? How could she be near him?

She finally got up and went to the place where they first met, *The tree; I'll go to the tree.* She slipped on her blue robe and her slippers. Outside, it was chilly but not frigid. The harvest moon lit her way to the tree. El leaned against it, her forehead pressed against the bark, with her arms wrapped partially around it. "Oh, Goldie," she whispered, "Where are you? I miss you so. Please come back to me."

A voice behind her caused her to jolt. It said, "Miss Eleanor, I'se sorry but Mr. Goldie can't come no moah."

El turned to see Cheche looking at her with soulful eyes.

"All right, Cheche. If you know so much and you've got the mojo, tell me why, Cheche, why?"

"Jes look at the song; it'll bring you along. Find some people you know; they'll have something to show. Tho yo mamma can't say; when she wants somethin' she'd pay."

Without another word or clue as to what her words meant, Cheche ran away. El didn't chase after her, what was the point? She walked back into the house and went to bed, even more determined to leave in the morning. When Cheche was done speaking, nobody could get anything more from her. But this time, though El tried to dismiss Cheche's mojo rambling as rhyming nonsense, it floated around in her mind until she finally drifted off to sleep.

The next morning, El got up as the sun rose and before Mama Tippi came to the house to fix breakfast. She took the ice cube tray out of the fridge, popped out the chunk of ice with the diamond ring and quickly melted the ice in the pot of boiling water she put on the stove. She spooned out the ring, turned off the burner and slipped the ring in her pocket. She then searched the house for cash Elma liked to stash in odd places. She double checked pockets in Elma's purse and for cash hidden in drawers, finding about five hundred dollars and some change. Not a lot for what she intended to do, but enough.

She left her one extra copy of Goldie's record on the table with a note for Mama Tippi. *I'll always remember how good you were to me. So, I want you to have this record, one of the original cuts. I know you'll always treasure it. I haven't found the only extra copy Goldie had, so please take good care of this one.*

Finally, after filling the car with her belongings, she grabbed the car keys and put them in her purse along with Mr. Tunstall's contact information. She also made sure the record, the music contract, and their marriage license was in her purse. It could end up that Mr. Tunstall would be owing her money from Goldie's record. She cringed; she'd rather Goldie be the one to get it.

At five a.m. El walked down the front porch steps of the Tollar plantation one last time. Re-living her mother's attack which flashed through her mind, she put her purse on the passenger's seat and got into the driver's side of the Buick.

As she backed out of the driveway, she turned on the radio, hoping to hear Goldie's song playing again. As if a sign from God, the mellow sound of Goldie singing *Reelin' Feelin'* brought tears to her eyes. All that happened in the past few weeks flooded her brain, her marriage, Memphis, her husband not returning, her mother's death, Cheche's mojo predictions. Worse yet, the predictions in Goldie's song seemed to be coming true. The mojo? It gave her goosebumps.

Casting those thoughts aside as superstitious, she pressed the accelerator as she drove down the dirt road away from the Tollar Plantation. The car moved forward faster, and she sped away from her past. She focused on her baby. El made a silent vow not to turn into her mamma as she rested her hand on her stomach. Except for continuing her search for Goldie, everything in her life was going to change. Everything!

Chapter 12

Sheriff Hunter Harley leaned back in his office chair and closed his eyes after studying the documents laying on his desk. It had been a long week. He'd sent Rocconi to the basement of the courthouse where they stored old police records to see if there was anything on Goldie Parsons. She came back that afternoon holding a worn manila envelope with the words, "Parsons, G. - Missing." written on it.

"I had to dodge a few cobwebs, but it was in an old file cabinet towards the back. Bunch of boxes in there, too," she told him when she put it on his desk, "we need to digitize that stuff. No telling what else is down there. I didn't even know that room existed."

"We're not cleaning up that mess. I think we have enough mysteries to solve today," he said as he opened the envelope, pulled out its contents, and studied the yellowed form filled out by former Sheriff Husk Grimes when Eleanor Tollar Parsons, his wife, reported Goldie missing.

"Rocconi, have you ever heard of an Eleanor Tollar Parsons?" Harley yelled toward her office next to his, as he read the contents of the form.

"No, but I have heard of the Tollar Plantation. Everyone knows that place. It is where the Delta Blues was born. You know it too, it's where those bones washed up," she yelled back.

"Isn't that convenient? Come here and look at this." He held up the report and pointed out details on it. "Eleanor Tollar Parsons reported her husband, who was Goldie Parsons, missing. She told Husk, Richard's grandfather, that Goldie had a gold tooth, and he was wearing a purple Zoot suit missing one button. Husk noted that it wasn't enough to go on. The record stopped there."

Rocconi pointed out, "A Zoot suit, huh? Those were popular with blues players in the 1940's. They tended to be flashy; it helped to get them noticed on the music scene. It was a sad state of affairs back then, but they never looked very hard or long for missing black men in those days. Besides, look at the date it was written up, December 9, 1941. My granddaddy told me World War II downplayed everything else that was going on after Pearl Harbor, even in Cleveland."

Harley double checked the envelope and continued, "There is no follow up information. They never found Goldie or even bothered to try."

Hunter closed his eyes again. He struggled to line up his image of Goldie with the remains found by the Sunflower River. Was this the same person? He did feel as if he was getting to know Goldie Parsons. After all this came up, Goldie had become someone who was flesh and bone.

Hunter was more than familiar with Goldie's songs. Deputy Chan, a big fan of blues music, took classes at Delta State University about the history of the blues. He liked to tell Hunter what he'd learned and he played Goldie's two songs on his CD player over and over. Hunter didn't care much for that type of music, so he'd drown it out with Hank Williams songs whenever he could. Hunter and Chan had a running battle, especially when they were on patrol together. Each one would switch radio stations all the time.

This was another reason Hunter hoped those were Goldie's bones that had washed up along the Sunflower River. In some ways, Goldie was revered almost like a mythical figure simply because he disappeared. If the man was officially declared dead and buried, the mystery of his disappearance would most likely dissipate and so would the long lasting attention to his music.

Hunter learned the next day that not a single professional in the Mississippi Delta was capable of examining the remains. So he sent Chan out to the scene, now guarded by Delta State University campus guards, to take photos of the crime scene that remained still untouched along the river.

After attaching the photos to the email to the medical examiner in Jackson, MS and receiving no response, his last chance was to contact his friend, the man who got him this job in Cleveland, Richards Grimes. Once he gave Richard a call, it was a matter of minutes before the Jackson Police captain phoned apologizing for not getting back to him sooner and telling him the forensics team would be on their way to Cleveland in the morning.

Though the captain had originally put him off, Harley was determined. If the body that had washed up was Goldie Parsons, he intended to find out. This wasn't going to go unsolved like the case in Texas. He refused to fail again. Because Richard told them the bones might be Goldie's, he won. Maybe now they'd get some results.

At ten a.m. the next morning, Hunter drove into town from the Shackem Up Inn, full from a breakfast at Levenia's place, and the first thing he saw was a green Prius parked in front of his office. *What have we here? The Green Peace Division?* Then he saw a lanky young man dressed all in black with horn-rimmed glasses outside his office and he sized him up. *They must have sent me someone fresh out of college. He can't be thirty years-old. Bet he doesn't weigh a hundred and fifty pounds dripping wet.*

After parking next to the Prius and noticing the size of its small tires, Hunter wondered how long it would be before he'd have to pull that little car out of the mud somewhere in town. He got out of his car and when he got close enough, he offered his hand to the young man in a shake, then ran his other hand through his hair. His heart wasn't in his actions. He thought, *I wasted a favor on this?*

The young man pushed his glasses up on his nose as he stretched out his hand and grasped Hunter's limply. *Not a good sign*, Hunter thought. Through a mouthful of braces, the man said, "I'm, er, Percy Calhoun, they sent me from Jackson."

Before Hunter could introduce himself, the passenger side door of the Prius popped open and another man stepped out, his foot caught on the door frame and he almost slipped to the ground before catching himself. Hunter cracked a smile as he noticed the man's baggy Jeans full of holes were too long for his five-foot four inch frame. While he didn't look professional, the Nikon camera around his neck indicated something different. Percy, with his unusually high voice hindered by the braces, said, "This is my photographer and assistant, JoJo Browning." Hunter had to remind himself to never judge a person too quickly.

"Sorry you caught me eating, Sheriff." JoJo held up a half-eaten doughnut. "We left early this morning and needed to stop and get a bite. The shop in town makes the best doughnuts!" After JoJo finished, he wiped his hand on his pants and reached out to shake Harley's hand.

Trying not to show his disgust, Harley complied, but he wiped his hand on his pants to remove the crumbles. "I'm Sheriff Harley, call me Hunter, and I'm on a hunt, ha, ha. I need your help." JoJo and Percy both grinned, catching the pun that Harley made.

At the office, while Harley made a fresh pot of coffee, he filled in the two men about the bones, Goldie Parsons, and the victim's obvious murder.

JoJo's lip curled into a grin when Hunter finished, "Hell's bells. You mean we're talking about that blues singer? I heard his song on the way over here. What's the title? *Reelin' Feelin,'* right? I didn't know the guy was dead."

Hunter was quick to correct him, "We don't know that for a fact and this is why they sent you here from Jackson. If he lived a natural life, he is probably dead by now, but what if he died back then when he was reported missing? We need to find out. If these are his bones that were washed up by the river, he was murdered. If we do not find out who they belonged to, it will make the legend worse. People will always wonder. "

Percy's eyes widened. "Wow, what a story! He's got a voice as good as Elvis Presley. But I don't keep up with blues singers." He stretched to his full six-foot-three inches. "But they told us we've only got one day here. Let's get down to business. Where are the remains, Sheriff? My kit is in the car."

126

"We bagged and tagged the remains at the scene. Picked up every bone and bits of evidence we found in the area. You can see them at the morgue. We didn't want anything to decompose further, so we placed them where they cool the cadavers." Said Hunter, "We did leave the original scene guarded for when you guys arrive."

"Cool!" said Percy, "We will get back to you this afternoon."

True to their word, not long after Hunter returned from lunch at the Delta Diner, Percy and JoJo returned with a detailed report. Percy handed the sheriff a copy and went through the procedure verbally with the sheriff. "We photographed the remains from all angles and X-rayed them at the morgue. This is consistent with a .38 caliber-size bullet going through his skull from above his right eye and into his left ear. Looks like one went straight through his ribs into his heart, too. Didn't find the ones that were the cause of the wounds. They're probably at the bottom of that river. We'll check on this gold tooth."

Percy pulled the bag containing the tooth out of his pocket after it was removed from the skull, and held it up to the office light. "You know he had a perfectly good tooth underneath? He must have had it put on for show."

Hunter walked around his desk and reached for the evidence in Percy's hand. "Leave the tooth here and I'll check with Dr. Chan, my deputy's cousin. His great-grandfather was the dentist here then. Won might still have the old man's records--I hope." He knew Goldie was a showman, so the gold tooth didn't surprise him.

Percy hesitated for a moment, but after a stern look from Hunter, he handed over the plastic bag with the tooth and made a note on his evidence form. "It's not according to our policy, but we are so far away from the main office and you can get more information than I could. Don't tell anyone we let you keep this tooth. We will put it in the report as a note on the bottom. If anyone asks, you will have to give it back, okay?"

Percy then passed the report to Hunter and pointed where he needed to sign the document. "Here's the complete report. I warn you, DNA results can take a couple of months, if we have enough for a sampling." He shrugged. "We do have a problem, we need a living relative today to compare it to. Do you know of any descendants? Anyway, unless the body is Goldie Parsons, no one is going to care who this was or how the victim ended up like this."

Percy chatted while JoJo made his way toward the door. "Hey man, we need to start heading back to town," he said.

Percy nodded. He gave Hunter his business card, "You have any questions, email me or phone me. My contact information is on the card." He glanced at his smartphone. "Thanks for your time, Sheriff, and I hope we meet again soon."

In a loud voice, JoJo yelled from outside the door, "We gotta go, Percy!"

Percy hustled out the door on JoJo's heels.

Hunter grinned as he watched through the glass front window of his office as the green Prius headed down Main Street. He returned to his desk and focused his attention on the tooth. *Goldie had a wife, it seems. Did Goldie have any children? Or grandchildren?* Hunter wondered.

Hunter picked up the tooth and studied it for a minute, then he shuffled through the papers on his desk, re-reading the missing report Husk wrote years before. He realized a gold tooth was Goldie's signature, this was a bit of proof. Probably not many people got gold teeth back then. Goldie also owned a flashy purple Zoot suit, but it couldn't possibly still exist. If El was right and Goldie was wearing it when he was killed, it disintegrated in the river.

Goldie's guitar was probably his most treasured possession, but it wasn't mentioned in the report, where did it go? If someone had it today it would be worth a small fortune. But no one has claimed ownership. Hard for someone to hide something that valuable. Most people would sell it.

Hunter looked up at the old photographs taken back when the Mississippi River levee broke back in the 1920's and sighed. *Now the levee has broken again and flood waters are bringing this story to the surface. This has to be Goldie, but I still need more proof.* He checked the patrol roster to see when Deputy Chan would be in to work so he could talk to him about his uncle. What facts would the dental records reveal, if they still existed? Too curious to wait for Chan, Hunter took out his cell phone, looked up the number, and dialed Dr. Won Chan's office phone.

"Won, not sure if we have met, but I'm Sheriff Hunter Harley and I have an old case I need to talk to you about. Can you meet with me this afternoon if you don't have patients lined up?"

In a cheerful voice, Dr. Chan agreed to meet at two p.m. He even joked with Hunter that since they hadn't met before, it meant Hunter hadn't had his teeth cleaned since he came to town as their sheriff.

Hunter was stoic. One of the few things that made him nervous was a visit to the dentist. As he drove to Dr. Chan's office, he adjusted the rear-view mirror to check the condition of his teeth. He was relieved to see they were in good shape; they didn't look like they needed cleaning yet, but his addiction to coffee would require it soon.

With a limited practice because of Cleveland's small population and the 2008 recession, Chan was always looking for patients, but he wasn't going to get Hunter in the chair today. This was official business, something he hoped would produce results. As he parked the patrol car, he glanced towards the seventies style brick building the office was located in and had doubts. Would Won have kept records from his father's practice? If he did, would he have any reason not to share them? He'd soon find out.

When he walked in he found Won sitting behind his receptionist's desk with a laptop computer open. Dr. Chan looked up and commented, "Receptionist is out today and it's just me." He moved aside one stack of paper and looked up. "Good to see you, Sheriff. What can I do for you today?"

They shook hands. "Please call me Hunter." Won smiled and pointed to a chair, so Hunter sat opposite the dentist.

Hunter then looked towards an open door that contained an examination chair, drills, and spit cups. Glad he wasn't in that chair, he looked back at Won and stated, "Well, I imagine you have some patients scheduled, so I won't take up much of your time." He pulled out the plastic bag containing the gold tooth and held it up. "I know you are too young to recognize this, but it came from that body we found at the river."

Won whistled, and then nodded twice. "I heard about that. It's the latest gossip, you know. You think it's the blues singer Goldie Parsons, don't you?"

"We're not sure. That's why I'm here." He leaned forward letting his body touch the desktop. "I hope you kept all of your father's old dental records. Goldie might have come to your father to get this tooth put on or checked on. I was surprised to find that it was cosmetic, not to fill in a cavity."

Dr. Chan winked. "Sometimes things happen right on time. We got grant funds from the Mississippi Dental Association to digitize old dental records. They sent us a computer, a hard drive, and plenty of CDs to use for backup copies of the records. We hired Delta State students to do the work part time. I think they are up to 1940. What year did Goldie disappear?

Hunter thought back to the missing report, "In early December 1941."

Chan rose from the chair, "Then you are in luck! Come with me; the computer and the old records are in the back room."

He walked behind Dr. Chan to the set up in the back. *This is going to be really close.* When he spotted the row of cardboard file boxes in bags piled on the floor, he had more reservations. *Mice, silverfish, what else could have chewed on these papers?* He held his breath. Dust and mildew emitting from the records caused him to sneeze.

Won opened a bag and pulled out one box with November, 1938, typed on a 3x5" card taped to the front. "This is the oldest record I have." He flipped through the other folders in the bag. "No Parsons here. Oh, are you sure he got the tooth here?"

"I'm not sure of anything. I'm just hoping to get lucky. I know many black blues players in those days had a nomadic lifestyle, never staying in one place long. I thought if he had some dental work done here, you'd have a record, maybe the mention of the work including the gold tooth."

Won looked up at Harley "Well, we're Chinese. Our policy always was to serve everyone, even though white folks frowned on it back then. Hmm, unless black people had a toothache, they didn't usually come to dentists." He pulled out another box from a bag and he could see where insects had chewed some of the pages. "Oh, we're going to have some damage here, I'm afraid." Corners of folders looked nibbled by mice and when he flipped to the "P's", the tops of files, where the names would have been written, were missing completely. He pulled them all the way out of the box.

Hunter's heart skipped a beat when he spotted part of a name on one folder. "Let me see that folder," he said. Inside, he found notes of a dental procedure to secure one gold eyetooth that had become loose! "Bingo! I think this is it. Can I look at this file?"

Hunter showed the note to Won and then he stared at the folder but could only make out three letters--*ons*. The other letters were missing due to the strategic munching of mice, and the top of the file was gone. Hunter sucked in his breath and didn't say the curse word he was thinking.

Bringing the file closer to his face to see if he could figure out more of the letters, Hunter said, "Now, if we can just prove this record was Goldie's, we can identify our victim." He shook Won's hand again. "Keep looking, Won. If Goldie came here once, he may have come again. Meanwhile, I'm taking this to the office and studying it. Then I'll call that medical examiner in Jackson and see if he can elucidate this anymore. You never know, Won. Nope, you never know." He strutted out with a broad grin on his face and a lot of determination circulating in his brain.

Deputy Zita Rocconi had suggested that Hunter make one other stop while he had the tooth in hand. In case they couldn't get any DNA evidence, and this was looking more likely by the day, or find a way to match the bones with someone, he needed something, or someone, for more conclusive proof. *How do I find out what happened to Eleanor Tollar?*

Hunter didn't believe in the mojo but Deputy Zita Rocconi was adamant that he speak to old Mama Cheche. He even wondered if it was another one of Zita's pranks. How could a black woman, the oldest person in town he was told, know about any of this?

He had also heard she had quite a collection of local historical artifacts. Zita told him that one of the ways she made a living was cleaning out old houses in exchange for selling the contents, but she didn't sell much. Instead, she hoarded things in the abandoned row houses that surrounded her own. No one dared to mess with her stuff, she put the mojo on it and the fear alone kept looters away.

Who knows what a woman like her might have come across and kept? Goldie's guitar was never found, but it could be in her possession. It could have ended up in a trunk somewhere. Maybe letters or photos of Goldie with Eleanor Tollar? A gun? Anything was possible. If anything about Goldie or this case still existed, Hunter was determined to unearth it. Texas failure be damned. This old, old case which no lawman before him cared about, and one that had baffled many a blues fan, was finally going to be solved--his redemption for the world to see.

Chapter 13

Mama Cheche snuggled under the Double Wedding Ring Quilt--one Grandma Dee's mother had made almost a century earlier--when she returned to bed that rainy night. But she couldn't sleep. She tossed and turned thinking about the hole and her gift of "the knowin' of what was comin,' expecting the mojo to materialize in the form of a vision. As she dozed an hour before daylight, it came. In a rush, all that Grandma Dee taught her worked its magic. Mojo took over her brain and her eyes rolled. Flood waters did "bring up the dead." Bones floated on shore, resting at the edge of the river. In the mouth area of the skull, she spotted a gold tooth.

Getting out of bed on shaky feet, her head still swimming from the vision, Mama Cheche ambled to the kitchen and made some coffee. She steadied herself with her willow stick, which she used only when feeling shaky, or on long walks. While listening to the coffee perk in her old percolater, she hand-cranked her record player she'd rescued from one of the houses she'd cleaned, put the needle in place, and flipped the switch. On it was the record Mama Tippi had given her. Goldie's voice cracked and then blared out for the thousandth time from the speaker below the turntable. She walked over to the sink washed out a mug labeled "#1 Mama" and swayed to the music, careful not to lose her balance. She was slow but she could still dance.

"I heard that song so many times, I could sing it," she said aloud as she poured a cup of coffee, dumped in four teaspoons of sugar and a swig of cream. "I'm feelin', reelin'," she sang off-key. "Too bad I can't carry a tune. Now, I'm the one reeling with all the memories that song brings back."

She sat at the kitchen table sipping from the mug, and stared out her window facing the cotton fields and the Sunflower river beyond, letting her thoughts drift to the past. By the time the record reached the end and kept making a scratching sound, the coffee cup was empty. Mama Cheche stared towards her front door where strange figures filled the open door frame between her kitchen and hallway. The skull reappeared and the gold tooth flashed at her; the rest of the pile of bones was smeared with mud. Mama Cheche's head swung backward. "Oh, it's the mojo. I stirred things up by poking around that hole. I saw it coming. The river done caused the dead to rise!"

The objects kept floating around as Mama Cheche's thoughts drifted back to a day when things happened that she never revealed to a soul. She was ten years-old and hiding behind the same tree where Eleanor and Goldie met. She saw Goldie in the distance, near the river, alone that evening, or so she thought. The gossip about their mixed marriage hadn't spread everywhere yet, but it was bound to. All the black folks were going to be stirred up, even afraid. And if the white folks found out and wanted revenge, Goldie and his white bride would pay the price.

Her thoughts were interrupted when she saw Goldie taking huge steps away from something or someone. Cheche knew something was wrong. Then she heard someone call out, "Goldie, stop. I've got something for you. Something you can take to that little white wife you got." Though his dark purple suit helped him to blend into the dark, it looked like he was headed to her home.

Mama Cheche squeezed her eyes shut and refused to let the grim scene that followed take over her consciousness. But some of it forced its way into her thoughts. She'd peeked around the tree again to see Grandma Dee pull Goldie to his feet and drag him along with her as she walked to the Sunflower River.

A heavy cough brought Mama Cheche back to reality. The figures disappeared. She pushed on the table to get to her feet. Taking baby steps, she made her way to the record player and picked the needle up and put it in its rest. *It's time. I'm old and I'm sick. Not long for this world. I can tell my story now. Nobody's alive who'd want to harm me. I managed to get educated by reading that set of Harvard*

Classics Mrs. Eleanor gave mama and me for sitting with her mamma before she died. Got respect for speaking proper English, but I sure didn't learn everything. I had to look up the word opsimath when the preacher called me that one day. it was a compliment not an insult like it thought. But that's the way I learned. Life is different now for the better. Things have also changed between blacks and whites, even concerning mixed marriages." She had another coughing spell but her thoughts continued to flow.

All in all, I've had a good life. Made my way cleaning houses. Got me some pretty good things when I cleaned out some for people moving. Had me a baby even though I never had a husband, didn't need him, and I raised her by myself. Mama helped till the day she died. Gave my child my maiden name Brown, too. She never married and never changed it to something fancy. She sucked in her breath. *Now all that's in the past. Mama's gone and Tippiny is a big city lawyer, lots smarter than me and making a fortune. I rarely see her. Won't do any good to moan about that.*

My revelation about what happened to Goldie won't help anybody, either, but I've got to get right with God before I die. If I don't, nobody will ever know the truth. Miss Zita told me to talk to this new sheriff if I knew anything. I know plenty, but nothing much about this sheriff. Now they've found those bones, Goldie's bones. I bet he'll be checking with me soon. I better tell him about that sales slip I found in Mrs. Elma's chiffarobe, too.

Chapter 14

While pulling her green dress over her head and sizing up her reflection in an old mirror from the big house, Mama Cheche considered how much she should trust this Sheriff Harley, a man the mojo told her had an uncertain past. He could accuse her of the crime and arrest her. It made her cautious and she wasn't sure if she'd trust him at all, not yet. Zita Rocconi said he'd come by soon and that "He's a good man," but she wasn't so sure.

She pulled a raggedy Whitman's candy box from the back of her chiffarobe, another relic from the big house long abandoned, slipped off the brown twine, and took out a pile of yellowing letters. The oldest one, postmarked March 30, 1942, Mobile, Ala., was on top. She slipped it out of the cut on the side of the envelope, unfolded the pages and read it again:

Mama Tippi,

I may not believe in Cheche's mojo, but even as a teenager, I can see that she is wise. And I do trust your daughter and you. You practically raised me. So I'm reaching out to you to see if you have heard anything about Goldie. You see, I'm expecting his baby and I need him so bad.

If you know anything, I'm staying at a boarding house and you can leave a message for me at this phone number. Don't tell anyone, please.

GOLDIE'S Wife, El

There was no return address, so Mama Tippi only knew where El was from the postmark. She hung her head. It was a hard secret to keep, but how could it have helped El? Even though she couldn't tell her about Goldie, mama still wanted to at least respond to Miss Eleanor. She owed her that much, but she just couldn't do it.

The next letter came after Eleanor's baby was born. Inside was a two-dollar bill. It said:

Mama Tippi,

I realized you didn't have the money to call me, but I haven't had any either. No need to go into detail about how I survived but I had a baby girl at a charity hospital. Little Ellie is four months old now and beautiful. She has her daddy's big brown eyes and wavy red hair. I love her so much.

Enough about that. I hate to leave Ellie with a babysitter, but I had to go to work. I took that new test and got my GED and I have a job at Brookley Field now. I'm saving money to go back to Cleveland and Memphis and look for Goldie. I went to Mon Luis Island, where Goldie told me he was from, and nobody there has heard from him. But with the war causing gas rationing, I don't know if I can make any trips. Anyway, I have to earn some leave first.

If you hear anything, anything at all, about Goldie, please, please let me know. Here's my number at work; call between 8 a.m. and 5 p.m. She gave a phone number. *The two dollars enclosed should be enough for at least one call.* This one was signed, *HIS Wife, El.*

Mama Tippi slipped on her green shoes; she always wore earthy colors. Even though she didn't have any information she'd reveal about Goldie, she'd gone downtown and made a call from a phone booth. But they didn't put her through to Eleanor. "Sorry," a man's brusk voice replied, "I can hardly hear you, but no Mrs. Carson works here." He hung up before she could correct the name. When she tried to call back, the phone quit working, but it took her money. She'd left in tears, once again with no money. Even if she'd protested to the phone company, it was unlikely that they'd have listened to a black woman or have given her a refund. She was out of luck.

Mrs. El probably thought Mama Tippi had spent the money on herself because she didn't write for quite a while. The next letter was a year later. Eleanor let Mama know she was disappointed but admitted she had no one else to turn to, so she was trying again. Mama Tippi looked at it, recalling how sad it made her to receive it. Miss Eleanor said she'd saved her money and her leave but couldn't get enough ration stamps for gas to make the trip she planned. So she pleaded with Mama to call her, offering to pay her for checking around to see if she could find out any news of Goldie. She also asked if maybe Cheche could call. She even condescended a little about the mojo, asking if Cheche had any "feelings" in that regard. She said she didn't want her baby to grow up without a father. Before closing, she made a statement that made Cheche shudder when her mother read it to her: "We don't know our fate. If anything happens to me, what will happen to Ellie?"

Cheche could still feel the chills that remark caused, knowing she couldn't help. *I know the truth and know it well, but there are things I don't dare tell that became* her mantra each time she felt the mojo taunting her. It helped her keep silent about her secret.

The next time a letter came, the envelope had a return address, a post office box. mama Tippi could manage to get a stamp, so she did. Before replying, she wondered what in the world she could say. Nothing. Still, she scrawled a note saying she wished she could help, asked about the baby, and mailed it to the post office box.

Miss Eleanor wrote back expressing disappointment but asked Mama Tippi, and Cheche, to "keep trying--something may come up."

Mama Cheche put the stack of letters her mother gave to her aside. All those years and exchange of letters amounted to nothing but idle talk, except the one time El came alone to look for Goldie. She stayed with Mama Tippi, Cheche and her little girl Tippiny two days but was out searching for information about Goldie all day and half the night. And they played Goldie's record many times. When she left, she gave Cheche a gift. "This is a button from Goldie's Zoot suit," she said. "I want you to have it as a memory of him." Cheche put it in her mojo bag with her Father stone, the one her grandmother gave her.

Cheche sighed. One day, the truth would come out and she hoped to be the one to reveal it. She picked up her purse, straightened her back as much as her eighty years would allow and walked out the front door.

But she didn't get far. The heel of her shoe caught on the bottom step and Cheche tumbled onto the ground in a curled up pile, blood spewing from a cut where she hit the bannister. She moaned, "Help me, somebody please help me." Before anyone responded, she fell unconscious.

***

Shaking her head in an effort to clear it, Mama Cheche reached for the bannister and pulled herself up. She staggered up the steps and managed to open the door, and made it to the living room where she plopped into an overstuffed chair. Her head was spinning. When she rubbed her forehead and felt a wetness, she looked at her hand and saw blood. After feeling the area and finding the blood seemed to be drying up, she ignored it.

Questions circulated in her brain. How long had she been unconscious? Where had she been going? Who did she want to talk to and what did she want to tell them? Nothing was clear. Then people from her past found their way into her consciousness.

First, there was Wylie. He'd come back to Cleveland and performed at the juke joint, bragging that he'd made a hit in Memphis. By then, Cheche was twenty years-old and she sat in the audience. What struck her was his reply when someone asked about Goldie. "Oh, Goldie was a flash-in-the-pan. He only made it big with that one record because of me. I got him the contract with Tunstall. But we got rid of old Goldie." Then he'd amended his statement. "Oh, I mean, he went missing. But he neva woulda been nothin' if he hada stuck around. Music has to be yo whole life if you wanna be famous and rich. Goldie didn't care that much. He wanted a wife and a family. He'd of neva made it as an entertainer."

Next, thoughts of Eli rambled around in her brain. Cheche had seen him around town several times during the years, but one time, shortly after Goldie went missing, stuck with her. He'd cornered her asking where he could go to take guitar lessons, saying, "I can catch onto anything pretty quick. I think I could be a star. All I need is a good teacher. I bet I could learn to sing, too."

When she asked if he had a guitar, he'd replied, "I sure do--a good one I found in the woods." With a wink, he added, "No tellin' who left it there. Maybe a famous blues singer who got run out of town for being drunk."

Next came Mrs. Elma Tollar, society matron. How she'd strutted around town bragging about Eleanor's marrying an attorney. "They'll be living in Memphis in a huge house. I haven't visited yet, but it's a two story mansion somewhere in the fanciest section of town."

If anyone brought up Goldie's name, Elma would reply, "He has disappeared and I'm quite sure we won't be hearing anymore about the likes of him. Good thing my Eleanor came to her senses."

Her head fell back and she opened her eyes. *What is the mojo trying to tell me? Sounds like any one of those three could be guilty of murdering Goldie. I've seen things and I've been given the signs. Now, all I have to do is put the puzzle together.*

The flashbacks of her life frightened Mama Cheche. She'd heard this happened sometimes when a person was dying. Her eyes shut as she leaned her head against the pillowed back of the chair. She strained to remember where she had been going and why. But she couldn't. Her brain cleared of all thoughts and despite efforts to remain awake, she drifted off to sleep.

The next thing she heard was a banging on her door. Mama Cheche called out, "I'm coming," but when she tried to stand she fell back into the chair. She rose again, steadied herself for a minute, and then went to the front door and cracked it open.

"Sheriff Harley, you're the last person I expected to see." A thought struck her that he was the one she'd planned to visit before she fell. "This is a coincidence," she said, "I was just on my way to your office. Then I fell…"

He looked at her head. "I knew something was wrong. I saw the blood on the steps." He looked at her wound. "You've got a bad cut there. Are you okay? Should we call the paramedics?"

"No, they'd take me to a hospital and I ain't dying today. I think I'm okay." She cocked her head. "But what are you doing here? I heard you usually have lunch at the Delta Diner at this hour." It was a small town and word spread fast. She didn't invite him to her home, bad mojo to do something like that, so they stood in the doorway and she leaned against the frame.

Hunter squared his shoulders. "Well, we've found a body, bones actually, down by the river. Flood waters washed it ashore. Deputy Rocconi thought you might help."

Mama Cheche nodded. "I knew about that." She didn't explain how.

"This will come as a shock. It may be Goldie Parsons."

She flinched, trying to fake her ignorance of Goldie and the situation. "Goldie? He's been gone for almost sixty years. Why do you think it's him?" She racked her brain. *I can't think straight, but wasn't it something about Goldie I planned to tell? The truth. The song. Oh, dear God! Flood waters did reveal Goldie's body.* Mama Cheche swayed sideways.

Harley stepped into her door, grabbing her arm and steading her. Then still holding her arm, he led her to the overstuffed chair. "You need to sit down. If you won't go to the hospital, let me take you to the doctor. Who's your doctor?"

"No, no. Just let me be. I'll be alright."

"But you could have a concussion."

"Had one before and got over it." She looked up at him with a cockeyed grin. "And I've survived much longer than most folks." She shook her finger at him. "But I just don't feel like talking. Right now, what I need is some rest. So, why don't you come back tomorrow, Sheriff?"

"Okay, but I still think you need to get checked. If you won't let me help you, call a friend."

"Ha, ha. Now that would be a neat trick. I'd have to call the graveyard; that's where most of my friends are."

"I guess I can't make you. I will be back tomorrow, okay? I have to go to the office, but call me if you need anything." Hunter didn't like leaving her like this, but knew he wouldn't win this battle. Come back to fight another day. In the rush, he forgot to take off his hat when he came into her home, so he tipped the edge and walked out the door. His Stetson boots clicked on the hardwood floor.

When Harley left, Mama Cheche didn't call anybody. She was simply buying time to clear her head. And it was working. Little by little the mojo kicked in with the gold tooth, and the song. She remembered the past again and made a shrewd plan. How much she told the sheriff tomorrow depended entirely on what he told her first.

***

While she slept a memory replayed as a dream. Images formed and took shape. One was Grandma Dee who told her, "Come with me, Cheche. It's time to go." She followed her grandmother out of their row house and down toward the river. The air was thick from a heavy rain. More bad weather was coming. Cheche held her grandma's hand as they walked closer to the river.

"He's here somewhere, Chile. Look for him." Grandma Dee squinted in the dark. Then a man's gasp of pain directed her ears toward a small, huddled mass next to the river.

Cheche caught her breath. It was Goldie, covered in mud and bloody. It didn't look like he could survive.

Grandma Dee stooped down and cradled him in her arms.

"You warned me; I should have listened," he cried as she rocked him in an effort to ease his pain. "It hurts so bad. I'll never see my El again."

"Son, we both sufferin.' Our time has come. She stared at the river, churning and grinding, in harmony to his fading breaths. "Let's go to the river, Goldie. We won't let others claim our deaths. We'll own what is ours."

As Goldie attempted to get to his feet, he slipped in the mud, and a dollar bill fell out of his Zoot suit pocket. Cheche picked it up out of the mud and blood and held it out to him. He shook his head, tears running down his pale cheeks. "I don't have any use for it now. Keep it." He glanced towards Grandma Dee as the rain came down and the Sunflower River beyond overflowed its banks. He said, "That river's calling me, too."

With his last strength, Goldie fell to his knees, grasping where the blood ran out of his body, and crawling toward the bank of the river with Grandma Dee at his side. She pulled him along when he paused, encouraging him to take just one more step to watery freedom.

Cheche's eyes followed them as they both entered the waves, finally realizing what was going on, she watched them going deeper and deeper into the river water. Then Goldie called out, "I ain't a Christian!" In shock, she knew there was nothing she could do.

Grandma Dee replied, "Now you are. The Devil didn't get your soul! You're baptised in this river. You're born again. Let's go home, Goldie."

In a flash of light that appeared from nowhere, Cheche saw old eyes stare into young ones. Then the two sank into the river and never came up.

It was three a.m. Jolted awake, Mama Cheche's head was splitting in two pieces. "Oh-h," she moaned, "I've got to get a couple of aspirin." When she took a bottle from the medicine cabinet in the bathroom something else fell out. It hit the floor with a ding. She tried to bend over to pick it up but her head was spinning. So she stooped down slowly and retrieved an object wrapped in tissue paper. Taped to the top was a note with misspelled words, written in her grandmother's handwriting:

Cheche--whn you reads this, it ll be time for you to fin my old mojo bag. It be kinda like a luckie charm. Maybe like the rabit foot folkes carie for good luck. Thes things are fo' you. My grandmother who I name afta give it to me. My time up soon, so I passes it on. You gots the mojo, so I give it to you. It kin protekt you, cauz you needs it.

I gots a felin it'll hapin when sumthin big is goin on. I sees a death longe past, the levee risin and a body come up. Be carefil. Whatevah you do, don tell to many secrets. Bide yo time. Wate til a lady comes. She knows all.

I caint write much but I hopes it clear. I loves you chile.

Grandma Dee

Mama Cheche picked up the small bag, constructed of sackcloth with a piece of leather twine wrapped around the top. Inside the bag were three items. A note said they represented the Father, the Son, and the Holy Spirit. One of the items was a small, polished stone with "D" inscribed on the flat backside of it. She'd seen Grandma Dee fondle it in times of stress, or during any crisis. All these years, she'd wondered what happened to it. It was a memorial stone, passed down from the first days her people were brought here. Years ago, Grandma Dee had explained to her that the chosen object represented the Father. It was magical and it could protect her and the family.

Her eyes widened as she looked at the stone in one hand and then at the medicine in the other. She hadn't taken the aspirin, but her head had stopped pounding. Holding up the plain brown stone, she looked in the mottled mirror of the medicine cabinet and said aloud, "This stone must be magic; the mojo is working." Drum beats followed by the words "Don't tell," echoed in her brain. Just when she'd psyched herself up to confess all that she knew, all this had to happen. First, she fell down the steps; then, after all these years, the stone appeared with this warning. Mojo.

The dream. The second item was the button from Goldie's Zoot suit that Eleanor had given her. How did it get in this bag? Did it represent the Son? She took it from her old bag and put it in the new one

Then there was the third item. Stuffed in the bottom of the bag she found a pocket-sized notebook with writing so small she couldn't read any of it. What did it all mean? Was it the mojo? Did it represent the Holy Spirit? She racked her brain but no clue would come.

Figuring things out would have to wait. The sheriff would be back soon. Right and wrong blended into a blurred line. What a dilemma. She put the other objects back in the bag, rubbed the stone and then laid it on top of her chest of drawers while she dressed. Glaring at it, she blurted out, "What in the world am I supposed to do or say? You sure better work your magic and tell me."

Chapter 15

The next morning, Mama Cheche readied herself to test the character of Sheriff Harley. What was this man made of? She had a mischievous side, her way of testing white folks to see if they were worth her time. It only surfaced when the situation was really important, and this was one of those times. She wasn't feeling any mojo today, so she had to use the common sense her mama taught her.

It was another rainy day in the Mississippi Delta, so when she looked through the window and saw Harley's police car drive up, she anticipated his knock on her door. She opened it to see him dripping wet from the continuing rain. She had made a point to wear her Kelly green scarf tied around her head and an old dress of Grandma Dee's of earthy colors with a sash to match as she'd anticipated his visit and she wanted to look nice for company, even if it was an official visit.

Hunter took off his hat as she opened the door wide. "How are you feeling today?" he asked. He pointed to the large scrape on her head from where she fell yesterday.

The blood had been cleaned off and her white hair braided down her back had no sign of it remaining.

"Oh, I'm just fine. It ain't my time yet." She winked at him as she escorted him to an old rocking chair and sat opposite him in the overstuffed chair.

Mama then leaned in closer to Harley who had a wary look on his face."Oh, Sheriff," she said, "I'm prepared to shake up your world. I do have some tales to tell you." She leaned back and waved her hands in the air, as if grasping at unseen things. "I have dreams and I have schemes. But I want to hear your story first. Is that body really Goldie's?" She then stopped her hands in mid-air and pointed a finger directly at Hunter.

He wasn't sure what was going on. He pushed back in the rocker, away from Mama Cheche. What dreams and schemes is this woman talking about? Harley didn't ask and wasn't sure if he really wanted to know. However, he still had an unsolved case and he was desperate. He explained in detail about finding the body and the gold tooth and that they were trying to get some DNA.

Mama Cheche laughed, "That gold tooth. Ha, no problem there. It probably is Goldie's. Not many black folks around here could afford something that flashy back then." She looked to the ceiling, jumped to her feet, and blasted out *Reelin' Feelin* off key.

Not knowing what to do, Hunter jumped to his feet as well, the rocker flipped backwards and turned over.

Cheche grinned as she steadied herself on her tiptoes. Then she made circles with her index fingers and pointed both of them at the sheriff. "Let him see what I see, and then please let me be."

Hunter was beyond confused. *How hard did she hit her head?* "What?" he asked.

"Follow me into the kitchen." Chehe walked in that direction, Hunter two steps behind her.

She then took a carving knife from the magnetic strip that attached it to the wall, held it up to the light streaming from the window, and stared at it.

Uh-oh, now she has a knife. Harley, not one to take unnecessary chances, backed away.

Mama Cheche smiled. "Easy, Sheriff, It's clean."

She walked over to the teal green 1950's style formica topped table, took an apple from a matching green bowl in the center, sliced it in half, and handed him a piece. He took a quick step forward to take it, and then backed off.

She continued to hum the song as she bit into her slice, but Harley wasn't about to take a bite of his. Crazy as she was acting, it might have been poisoned. She walked right in front of him, not intimidated by his size, and said, "If you come back in a few days, I may have something for you. Just maybe..."

"Just maybe...what?" he asked, but she raised a finger to cut off the conversation. She had distracted him enough to edge between Harley and the back door. When he stepped left, so did she; when he moved to the right, so did she. He scowled. He wasn't about to manhandle this old woman and physically move her out of his way. So he took the same steps a couple of times. After they did their little dance, she moved aside and let him pass.

Eager to leave, Harley stepped outside, but then stopped. Was she playing with him? Distracting him from what she really knew? He turned to ask, "Do you have something of Goldie's, Mama Cheche? Maybe something we could use to check his DNA?"

"I said no such thing. Just maybe...I do, or maybe I don't. Come back if you want to know." She needed him gone so she could look for that dollar bill. But she thought she'd spent it years ago.

Harley, still trying to be calm, checked his watch. He put his hat back on and said, "Now, Mama Cheche, I don't have much time--crimes to solve, people to see--can you cast any light on this case?"

Why wouldn't he leave so she could look for that damn dollar? *Maybe if I tell him to get me something he'll go away*, she thought. "You know, Sheriff, my flashlight's broken. If I had one, maybe I could find a few things."

All Harley wanted was to get out. He went to his car and got an extra flashlight and gave it to her. " He tipped his hat and tried to help one more time. "Mama, I still think you need to see a doctor, or go to a hospital. Maybe you did have a concussion."

She glared at him. "If I did, Sheriff Harley. It's mine, all mine."

***

Outside, Harley pulled his hat tighter on his head. It was still drizzling and he wished he'd worn a raincoat. Confusion consumed him. *What the Hell? That wasn't mojo. Does she have a concussion or is this woman nuts?* He needed to find out more about Mama Cheche. Was she really wacko? Or was she toying with him, playing him for a fool? Ha, maybe she was smarter than he thought. Only one person might know. He got into his car and headed for the diner to talk to Levinia. As he turned the key in the ignition a thought struck him: *Mama Tippi managed to get me going. Maybe she's sane and I'm the one who's nuts.*

Chapter 16

Mid-morning patrons in the diner sipped on coffee, staring out the window at the rain coming down harder by the minute. When Hunter arrived after stopping by his Pink Palace to pick up his wallet he'd left behind, he recognized two national reporters and cringed when a few people waved and one called out, "Mornin,' Sheriff," You think this rain's ever gonna stop?"

As Harley hung his wet hat on the coat rack by the front door and took off his raincoat, he replied, "Only God knows. But I hope that happens before the whole town's flooded." Relieved that the reporters didn't react to that exchange, he sat in his usual spot by a window. When Levenia, with her perpetual smile, came bearing a cup of black coffee, he asked, "You got a minute to sit and talk?"

Levenia surveyed the room. "Sure, we're not busy right now. Missed you at breakfast this morning. You got some mystery on your hands! I bet the Grimes family are beside themselves by this old case being stirred up. Any new leads on whose bones those are?"

Hunter sighed and glared at his coffee, "Not really. But I made a couple of visits to Mama Cheche and that's what I want to talk to you about." He shook his head. "The day before yesterday, she had a fall and said she couldn't talk. She told me to come back. Yesterday, I returned to find her acting mighty odd. Crazy like. Pulled out a knife, like she was trying to scare me. All she did was cut an apple in half. I think she knew all about those bones and what we'd found so far. Then she said she might have some information but she wouldn't tell me a thing--except to come back again and maybe she'd "have something for me."

With a big grin, Levenia slapped her knee and leaned back. "She's putting you on, Hunter. She does that sometimes, and she's good at fooling people."

Hunter wrinkled his brow. "But she did have a fall and it left a scrape on her head, I saw it. She could have a concussion and she wouldn't take my advice and get it treated. She refused to go to the hospital or the doctor."

"Naw, Mama's a tough old woman. If anything, she'd rather work the mojo on it. I bet you two dinners she's just playing a trick on you."

"No bet; you're probably right, and I don't like to lose. I just don't want to be responsible if anything happens to the old lady." He pulled out his iPhone. "I didn't get anywhere with Mama, but maybe you can be of some help. Just keep what you know quiet for now, okay?"

After she nodded, Hunter showed Levenia photos of the remains found by the river. This included a close up of the mouth, and the gold tooth. "Do you recognize this? Do you think there is any connection between Mama Cheche and Goldie Parsons?"

"Sheriff! I hope I don't look so bad you think we're the same age. Mama Cheche's about thirty years older than I am. First time I heard of her I must have been about five years-old. Funny, I overheard my mother telling my daddy she'd run into Mama Cheche at the grocery store. She said, 'That woman was arguing up a storm with the cashier. She had a large rotten potato in her hand and said she wanted another one, that it was rotten the day before when she bought it. Trouble was she didn't have a receipt. Well, they argued until a manager came over. Mama told him he was going to wish he'd given her quarter back to her. Ha, ha, Mama threw the potato at his feet where it split apart and oozed juice all over his tennis shoes. Mama pointed at him and called out *You'll hear more from me with my mojo.*'

"My daddy asked, 'Did you hear that anything bad happened to that man?' Mama said, 'It sure did. When he escorted Mama Cheche to the door and opened it, it fell back on him, and broke his nose.'" Levenia twisted a curl of her hair. "Of course, we don't know that the mojo worked, but lots of people believe in it." She squinted. "But not you, huh, Sheriff?"

"No, but let's move on. What else can you recall, tell me, even if it's just, er, gossip."

Levinia shook her finger. "Oh, I've heard lots of gossip. This diner is a breeding spot for it, more so than a beauty shop, believe it or not. Do you know men gossip as much as women? Oh, yeah, I can tell you some stories I heard. But where to start?" She closed her eyes and then opened them wide. "You know what? Maybe twenty years ago Eli Tarsi came in here late one evening. I could tell he'd been drinking; he was stumbling around and I saw him load his coffee with whiskey. He was yelling, 'I oughts be a rich man, but I'm not'. He took out a little ragged notebook and turned to a page. 'Got my record right here. That damn Mrs. Tollar died before she paid me the rest she owed me for the work I did for her. If she wasn't dead, I'd be going after her to get it.' He slammed the exact cost of his bill on the counter, gulped down his coffee and left. I sure was glad; Eli seemed like the type who could get violent."

Hunter bit his lip. Even if this Eli Tarsi was dangerous, all that Levenia reported was just talk. *Did he hurt, or even threaten, anybody? I wonder if there's any proof or details in that notebook. Doubt if we could find it, though.* He moved on. "What about Goldie? Know anything?"

"Yeah, maybe a little. Like everyone else in Cleveland, I've heard about the furor the mixed marriage caused, and I've listened to Goldie's song a thousand times, plus all the talk about his going missing." She leaned forward. "I can't substantiate this, but I heard that Eleanor, the Tollar girl, came back a couple of times looking for Goldie. She didn't stay at her old house, either. Abandoned it. Maybe too many unpleasant memories. They said she stayed with Cheche when she was here." She took a deep breath. "That raised some eyebrows. In those days, white folks didn't stay with black folks." She shrugged. "But Eleanor had married a black man, so I guess that changed the rules."

Levenia rested her chin in cupped hands and stared at Hunter. "You know, Mrs. Elma couldn't accept that marriage. It was the one time she didn't get her way, no matter how hard she tried. Eli spread word that she sent money to Goldie, trying to pay him off to leave Eleanor. But he never cashed the check if there was one. Probably tore it up. Bet his rejecting it made her livid. Wouldn't surprise me that when she couldn't break up that marriage, it caused her to have a stroke."

Hunter stroked his chin. "Have you ever heard anything about a fight or bad blood with Goldie?"

"Folks liked Goldie; he didn't cause any trouble with his own people and he kept his place with whites. Of course, when he started seeing that white woman, then feelings changed. I did hear he had a big argument with Wylie after he came back from Memphis. Not a real fight, no punches. They met at the Crossroads and the story goes that Wylie kept telling Goldie he needed to focus on his music, not on any woman, much less a white one. He had

Goldie going, trying to convince him to sell his soul to the devil for success. Sounded like Wylie had a scheme to team up and they'd both profit. Goldie was too much in love to give in. It seems that it all blew over. Geez, even if they'd found Goldie's body right away, they couldn't have questioned Wylie about it, he left town. That might make him a suspect, though." Levenia tapped the table. "But you can't question him now, either. Cheche said he passed away about ten years ago in Clarksdale. Playing the blues till the day he died."

"That would make it difficult." Harley cracked a grin. "Kind of ironic that they met at the Crossroads. Hmm, same place they say Robert Johnson sold his soul to the devil. Didn't sound like that disagreement would lead to murder, though." He shrugged. "But you never know. Any other ideas about who might have had it in for Goldie?"

"Eleanor's mama, of course. This is according to Eli. He also passed about twelve years ago, a weasel of a man, but when he couldn't pay for his breakfast here, he told some tall tales, so we'd let him hang around and eat free. The story goes that Mrs. Elma sprained her ankle when she fell on her front steps the day Eleanor left with Goldie. She couldn't get out of bed. She knew Goldie came back to Cleveland and she kept tabs on him through Eli. He bragged to people about reporting to her on a daily basis and he flashed around twenty dollar bills showing off. She must have paid him well for his spying. Seems like he was a big blowhard but a sneaky type. Roamed all around town day and night. After his mama died, he lost it. Before long they put him in a nursing home."

"Do you know how long it was before Mrs. Elma could walk again? Think she was involved?"

"That's the reason she couldn't have killed Goldie. She never left her house after her fall. She was barely hobbling around when she had that stroke. And it did her in."

The restaurant door opened and in walked Jenny Stein. Hunter stood, turned his back, and pulled out his wallet. He put a twenty dollar-bill on the table. "Gotta go. Thanks, Levenia. You've been a big help. One more thing. Did Eli have any relatives or close friends?"

"Good question."She scratched her head. "Let's see. I wouldn't say Father Jim at the Catholic Church was a friend, but he and Eli knew each other. Mrs. Tarsi was a devout Catholic, but Eli rarely went to church. If he went to confession, that conversation is sealed. Fr. Jim died last year anyhow." She cut her eyes upward. "You said you've already talked to the only person left that's not six feet under--Cheche. But, maybe you should try her again." She rose and stuck the money in her pocket. "As the old saying goes, 'If first you don't succeed...'" The phone rang and she hurried to answer it while calling over her shoulder as Hunter grabbed his hat and raincoat and sneaked out a side door, "Good luck, Sheriff. You're going to need it."

Hunter's luck didn't hold. Before he got within a mile away, he got a call from Deputy Chan to go to a six car pileup on the state highway. When he reached the scene, the fire engine was the first thing he saw. EMTs were taking away bodies. He counted two adults and two small enough to be children. Some people were being treated on the scene. The damaged cars and an eighteen-wheeler blocked all the eastbound lanes. Three of the cars had out-of-state licenses. It looked like they hydroplaned and skidded into the others. Bad weather moved in, making conditions worse. Working in the rain amidst thunder and lightning slowed down the process; it took all afternoon to clear the area.

By eight p.m., exhausted, and hungry from missing lunch, Hunter and his team headed home. They hadn't identified the victims, but he hoped none were locals. He was too distressed to talk to anyone else. To keep his sanity, everything had to be put on hold. But that wasn't going to happen. Two blocks from his Pink Palace, all the streetlights went off, so did the lights coming from houses. Except for the headlights on cars, Cleveland was dark. Hunter didn't care. He used his flashlight to find the front door, opened it and went straight to bed still clothed, and closed his eyes. He was instantly asleep.

Chapter 17

Mama Cheche had been pacing around in her row house for about half an hour when the lights went out. Another rainstorm was brewing and she saw a flash of lightning followed by a loud crack of thunder. She didn't know why the storm made her so restless but she blamed it on the mojo. She remembered the hole in the tin ceiling roof outside, so she went out on the porch, and aimed her flashlight at the spot made many years before. It looked the same, almost. The putty had pulled loose and drips of rain water landed on the wooden porch floor. *What does that mean? Is it a message?* Another flash of lightning followed by a clash of thunder made her whole body shake. It lit up the sky and struck close to the tree where Goldie and Eleanor met.

Mama Cheche rushed back inside and took her handwritten list of contacts from a kitchen drawer. With the cell phone her daughter gave her, she told it to call Tippiny's number. It was late into the night, but she needed to talk to her. When Tippiny finally picked on the tenth ring, she didn't give her mother a chance to speak.

Tippiny whispered, "Hello, Mama. Look, I'm at a dinner meeting. Could we make this quick?" Voices and music in the background almost drowned her out.

"Baby, the electricity's off; I hate it when the lights go out. And it's thundering and lightning something fierce. I don't like this, Tippiny, not at all. And I'm feeling something weird. It's not good."

"Mama, you know I can't do anything about that. Sounds like you're thinking about the mojo again. Nothing's really weird. You can get help. You're calling me on your cell phone, so I know it's working. Call the power company. It's on your list of numbers." She turned away from the phone. "Be with you in a minute, Shannon." Then she said, "I've got to go, Mama. I'll try to call you later." Click.

She ignored her daughter's advice. Calling the power company wouldn't help. All she'd get was a recording. Feeling slighted, Mama decided to go for help. She slipped on a heavy yellow raincoat, put her cell phone and the Father stone in her pocket, but forgot to take her umbrella.

In a daze, she ventured out into the storm, wind and rain whipped around her. Using the flashlight Hunter gave her, she followed the path from her home to the main road, acting oblivious to the storm's danger. The old path led her where it always had in the past, to the banks of the Sunflower River. She heard the water churning and mojo told her she was near where those bones had been discovered recently. She shivered and her heart skipped a couple of beats, but she continued on her way. Turning the flashlight in all directions, the bright beam flashing on tree trunks, tall grass, and brown mud, she surveyed the area. *Oh, mojo, you led me here. Tell me what I'm looking for.* No answer.

Then a flash of lightning revealed a pile of bone-like items at the river's edge. She walked closer to the river, feet sinking in the muck as she aimed her flashlight at the area and squinted. *Are those twigs or bones I'm seeing. Something oval. Small. Looks like a skull. Could it be Grandma Dee? Did she wash up too?* Wide-eyed, Cheche inched toward the pile. But she tripped on a fallen limb hidden by the dark and couldn't reach the spot. The stone fell out of her pocket and rolled out of her reach. Afraid she lost the phone, too, she reached into her pocket and grinned; it was safe. She pulled the flashlight close and dialed Zita's number that was in her contacts.

"I think I've found another body by the river, Zita."

"You're breaking up. I can't hear you. Is this Mama Cheche? Where are you?

"Yes, it's me. I'm down by the river, near where you found Goldie's--those other--bones. And I see some here. I..."

"What the hell are you doing there in the storm this time of night? Did you say bones?"

171

"I'll tell you when you get here. Don't ask questions, Zita. Just come. I've fallen and I can't get up."

"Okay, okay. The roads are slippery. It'll take me a while, but I'm on my way. Just hang on."

As Zita backed out of her driveway, she wondered what could happen next?

She then called Hunter, "Hello Sheriff."

He answered in a sleepy voice, "What's up?"

"Hate to awaken you," she replied, "but we have a situation." She explained the details.

"I was afraid of this. But we've got an edge. You know that flashlight I gave her? I put a tracker in it and linked it to my cell phone. I can tell you exactly where she is. We can't lose her! See you soon."

Damn it all, Hunter thought as he quickly got dressed and darted to his patrol car. Wheels were spinning as he brought up her location on his cell phone. *I need to get there as fast as I can. I don't want that old woman to die on me and take the secrets only she knows with her.* He hit the steering wheel with his fist. *But if this is just some of her mojo, I'm gonna be mad as hell.* When the car skidded into another lane barely missing an oncoming pick-up truck, he grasped the wheel with both hands. *If I didn't know better, I'd think Mama Cheche was turning her mojo on me.* He took a deep breath. *Can't let this long, tragic day get to me.*

He had to keep his senses to deal with what would probably keep him up all night.

Hunter turned onto Highway 8 just as he saw Rocconi pull in behind him, sirens flashing into the night. It relieved Hunter a little to know Zita could help him. His deputy was more efficient than most female officers he'd known. She also knew the citizens of Cleveland and could handle them better than he could. Hunter knew folks still considered him an outsider. It took a while for anyone to become accepted, even an officer of the law; the same was true of any small town. Trust had to be earned. Maybe if he could solve this case, that would do it. *And it would also erase my failure in Texas.* That case always surfaced; it stuck in his craw.

Hunter made it to the river first, followed closely by Zita. Both of them drove as close as they could get to the river without getting stuck. Zita with a flashlight and umbrella; and Hunter with the tracker on his phone directing them to Mama Cheche's location, rushed towards the river and finally spotted a figure on the ground. Zita called out, "We're coming, Mama Cheche." They sloshed through the mud in the driving rain and reached the woman's side. Zita did her best to use her umbrella to keep the rain off Mama Cheche's shivering shoulders. Hunter pocketed his phone, and reached under Mama's arms to try to lift her. "Try to stand and I'll get you out of here, Mama Cheche."

"No." Mama Cheche slapped away his hand. "I've lost my stone and I'm not leaving here without it." She pushed her hands in the mud around her while Zita kept the umbrella over her.

"What stone?"

"My Father stone." She got up on her knees, still holding onto the flashlight, and aiming it in all directions. "Grandma Dee left it for me and I just found it. I swear. I need it. I'm not going anywhere without it."

Oh, Lord. More mumbo-jumbo. Don't let this be happening to me. I've got to get this woman out of here or she'll die. Hell, if I get any more soaked, I might die with her. He tried again to lift Mama Cheche to her feet. "Let me get you to the car and I'll come back and find it."

Wriggling free with a strength that surprised Hunter, Mama Cheche cried out, "No, I have to find it myself. Don't you see? No, I guess you don't. But let me tell you, you don't want to mess with the mojo, whether you believe in it or not." She tried to step forward, but her knee gave way.

Hunter caught her and Zita met his eyes and knew they had to work with her if they were going to get her to leave. This old lady may have been obsessed with the mojo, but she wasn't senile. He needed to humor her until help arrived and could convince her to take refuge in the car. "All right," Hunter agreed as he took the flashlight from her. "If you let Rocconi get you to the car, I'll flash the light around and you point to the stone if you see it. By the way, I heard you spotted some bones, too. Let's see if we can find those."

When Hunter walked around the area, rain poured off the rim of his hat, shining the light here and there until he saw it hit a shiny object. "That's it!" Mama Cheche yelled. "Hooray!"

Before she could make a move, Hunter said, "You wait here." He handed Deputy Rocconi the flashlight. "Keep it aimed at the stone and I'll go get it." To his surprise, Mama Cheche didn't object.

As Hunter reached down to pick up the stone, he called back over his shoulder, "Do you see any bones? Is this where they were?" No reply. He retrieved the stone and walked back to where Zita had managed to get her into her patrol car. No bones. Only a few twigs and a broken limb. *Maybe that's what Mama Cheche saw and took them to be bones.*

When Hunter handed over the stone, Mama Cheche kissed it before putting it in her pocket. Zita stood by the door, umbrella still in hand protecting Mama from the rain. Hunter huddled close to check on the welfare of the two women. "Are you all right? Mama? Rocconi?"

"All wet's more accurate," Zita retorted. She whispered to Hunter. "Like it or not, I'm taking her to the hospital. She could have pneumonia and that would be the death of her."

Hunter nodded. "Go ahead and good luck. I bet you won't get her out of the car. That's a stubborn old woman. My bet's on her."

"No doubt. I need to get Mama Cheche to the....er, into some dry clothes. I will let you know what happens."

Hunter stepped aside; the rain had slowed to a drizzle, and tipped his rain-soaked hat. "Ten-four. I'm going to take a look around. I'll touch base with you in a while."

He watched Zita pull away and drive back towards the highway. Then he walked back to the river's edge. Hunter poked around the pile of twigs and the fallen limb, one that could have been mistaken for a leg. But that was all he found. Nothing really suspicious. No body parts. Mama Cheche's imagination had gotten the best of her. He headed back to his car. No need to make a run for it, he could hardly get any wetter.

He didn't dwell on the futility of this trip, but one thing tossed around in his brain. Mama Cheche was obsessed over that stone. What in the world was that all about?

***

When Zita helped Mama Cheche into her house, she offered to run a tub of hot water for her and help her bathe.

Mama Cheche scowled. "I'm perfectly able to take care of myself." She ambled over to the modified indoor bathroom Tippiny had installed in her row house with the first check she'd earned as a lawyer. Her heart fluttered and she sat on the side of the tub waiting for a little dizziness to pass. *I wish Tippiny lived here. I need her, but she is good to me. That check she sends every month helps me get by. I couldn't live on my Social Security.*

Zita called back with reassurance, "I know you are capable of taking care of yourself, but I'll wait for you. I have to be on duty in a couple of hours. Not worth trying to go home and get any sleep."

Mama poked her head out of the bathroom door. "Suit yourself." She pointed to the kitchen. "Make a cup of coffee, if you like. If you'd like to hear the other record of Goldie's--*My Light, My Star*, just turn on the record player."

The words spoke to hard-nosed Zita, secretly a sentimental romantic. *When I've got the blues, Your twinkle gives me a whole new view, You're my life, my light, my star* rang out in Goldie's mellow voice. Zita paused her coffee making to listen. Next came, *No time or space can keep us apart, You have won my heart, I need you, woman, right next to me, Oh, with you, I'm free.*

Zita teared up. *But you were kept apart and never free, so sad. Unless you're together in heaven. Oh, what happened to you, Goldie? And El? Will we even know?*

She poured herself a cup of coffee and squared her shoulders. *I can't let Mama see me crying, acting like a silly schoolgirl.* Drying her tears, she looked out the window and noticed the sun rising. She stepped outside to get a breath of fresh air and walked across the porch, glad the rain had subsided and her clothes had partly dried.

Then her foot hit something that she felt through her shoe. Stooping down, she picked up a small piece of hard, dried putty. "Now where did that come from?" On the porch flooded with bright morning sunlight, she looked around and then up at the ceiling. Zita squinted. *Am I seeing things? That looks like a hole.* There wasn't enough light to get a good look. *I'll come back later in the morning. But how in the hell did a hole get in this porch's ceiling and when did that happen?*

Zita heard Mama Cheche call her name and went back inside. Mama had filled two mugs with coffee and she put three day-old biscuits in a saucer on the table. "I bet you're hungry. It's been a long night." She tightened the sash on her bathrobe and pushed a strand of damp white hair behind her ear. "Thank you for rescuing me."

Just as they sat down at the table, Mama Cheche's cell phone rang; she retrieved it from her damp jacket and pulled it out of the pocket to answer it. The space in the row house was so small, Zita could hear a woman screaming on the other end of the line.

"Mama, this is Tippiny. Where have you been?" Without a pause for a response, she continued. "I met someone here in Washington, D. C. at this party, another attorney. Have you heard my messages? I've been trying to catch up with you for hours. he is a high ranking attorney; she has an in with all the congressmen. She is in a position to help me a lot. This is important. When she learned where I was from, she bombarded me with questions. She wants some information you might have.. We've been up all night…"

"You and me both, girl. Hold on, Tippiny. Who is this person and why do you think I'd know anything that would help her? Don't go trusting strangers."

"Give me time and I'll explain. It's a long story, but I'm good at summaries. I am a lawyer, you know." She chuckled. "Her name is Shannon Edwards. I was chatting away about being from Cleveland, Mississippi and small town stuff. She then pulled me to the side and asked all about Cleveland. I told her my mother lived there, and she got excited, mentioned Goldie Parsons, and said her grandmother always called her Goldie. She knew about his famous songs and the record, but not much else. Her grandmother died in a car wreck when she was about five years-old and her mother would never tell her anything about her background. All she knew was that her grandmother was from Cleveland. Her dad left when she was a baby and then her mother died of cancer the year she went off to college. She just wants to know about her roots. What do you know? Now don't start with that mojo stuff. Just give me the facts. What about that Tollar woman and the mixed marriage? Didn't she have a child and move away?"

Mama Cheche glanced over to Zita, aware that she was listening to everything, but decided it was time to share a bit of what she knew. "Eleanor Tollar did leave and she and Goldie Parsons got married in Memphis. He came back and disappeared. She came looking for him and found a dying mother. She left town when Mrs. Tollar passed. Your grandmother told me she had a girl and worked in Mobile at Brookley Field."

"Seems like I remember her coming back looking for Goldie, and staying with us."

Mama Cheche looked at Zita and saw her eyes go big in surprise.

Aha! So Eleanor did return to try to find Goldie. I'm learning something. But Zita heard Mama Cheche reply, "Yes, a long time ago," before she walked down the hall and into the bedroom with her phone.

She came back without it in about ten minutes. "I'm sure you heard most of that conversation. That woman Tippiny met wants to know about Cleveland. Maybe she thinks Goldie made lots of money on that record and she'll try to claim it. She may be in for a surprise. Money, ha! Black entertainers never got their due. They got gypped out of it by agents." She wiped a tear from the corner of her eye. "Funny thing, Tippiny never found out where I was when she tried to call earlier. She never even asked. I guess she's too caught up in her own world of legaleze."

Zita didn't do what she wanted--she resisted putting her arm around the woman. It may have seemed too familiar. Instead, she made the excuse, "I'm sure Tippiny is just too busy to think straight. But I'm sure she loves you, Mama."

"She's not too busy to think straight on the job. You know, she hardly ever loses a case. But, to be fair, I think she loves me, too. She does help me financially. Young folks just get their values all twisted."

"If you're okay, I've got to leave." It struck Zita that in Mama's sentimental mood she might reveal something, so she sauntered onto the porch and looked up. Pointing to the ceiling, she asked, "What in the world is that hole? Looks like a bullet made it."

Mama Cheche grabbed one shaking hand with the other, steadied herself on her feet, and paused before replying with a shrug. "Don't have a clue. Never saw it before." She squinted. "But be sure to tell the sheriff I found some bullets and a sales slip at the Tollar's house when I cleaned it out years ago." She turned and went into the house without a goodbye.

Zita froze for a moment but her brain remained awhirl. *Now my curiosity is really high. Soon as I get home, take a shower, and get into a dry uniform, I'll be back probing and questioning. Be ready, Mama Cheche, be ready with answers.*

Chapter 18

Peeking out the window until she was sure Zita left, Mama Cheche let the curtains fall back in place, then she took her damp jacket from the hook on the wall and retrieved the mojo stone from the pocket. She rubbed the smooth top, memories of her grandmother returning to her mind, and then laid it on the table to stare at it. "Grandma Dee, you'll have to help me with this one. I don't know what to do. Good Lord, people are coming at me from all sides. First, the Sheriff and Zita, then my daughter, next, it'll be that woman, Shannon."

"I know I've got to clear my conscience before I die. My heart could give way at any time. But how much do I need to tell?" She walked over to her record player and switched it on. Goldie's song blurted out, *Reelin' Feelin'.* "There's something in those lyrics that I've been missing all these years."

She reached the table and flipped over an old envelope, reusing the backside to write down notes. Using a pencil, she put down, *Look for the clues, Here in the blues.* She wrote down a few other lines and squinted at them.

"What that means is in the song somewhere; I feel it. I've just got to find out what it is."

Mama closed her eyes. "I've got a reelin' feelin' right now. It's close. The levee did rise." She bit her lip so hard it drew blood. "I know who killed Goldie, but I need proof. I feel in my bones that it's staring right at me. The answer is right on the tip of my tongue." She wiped the blood away with her finger, took the few steps to the front door and flung it open. The morning sun blazed over the cotton field. She could see a tractor preparing the ground for planting in the distance. The dust it kicked into the air made everything hazy.

On the porch, Mama stared at the hole and familiar drumbeats echoed in her ears. She covered her ears with her hands as if that would drown out the loud beat. "Grandma Dee," she screamed, "I know how that hole got there; and I know all about the murder; help me. You left the mojo stone for a reason. Tell me how to use it. My time on Earth is almost up. Please let me die with a clear conscience. I know they can't hang anybody for this crime. And I thought nobody could benefit from bringing a killer to justice. Then Tippiny called and she's bringing this strange woman here. Who is she? Should I tell them the truth? I'll have to prove everything. What do I do?"

She could still hear the music playing from inside her house. Mama listened closely again but nothing came to her. It was time to bring out at least one thing she had hidden for a long time. This would get their attention for sure.

She went back inside and switched off the record player. Opening the cupboard, she pulled out some heavy pots and pans. Behind them, a tattered rucksack held a large object. Removing its contents, she unveiled an old Gibson guitar. "Got this when I was clearing out and cleaning Eli's house when his kin put him in the nursing home. I know whose it is, but I can't prove that either. Yes, but it's almost time for me to give it to the sheriff. I need to do that soon." She walked back over to the table and looked at the other verses she'd written down, reading, *Now I'm reelin' and I've got a feelin'. I feel so blue; will it ring true?*

The rhymed couplet gave her a clue that the magic was working. Mama Cheche needed to rest so she sat in the stuffed chair and leaned back for a quick nap. Tired as she was, she didn't fall asleep right away. In a half-awake state three letters floated through her subconscious, forming the word *LIE*. It smacked of a revelation, but still was not clear. Exhaustion overcame her but it didn't obliterate Goldie's song which kept replaying in her mind, but it was stuck on two lines: *Eventually, Levees' floods redeem me. I'm reelin'.* That had come to pass. Bones had surfaced. But what to do about it? It transferred to her dreams and caused her brain to whirl. Her last thoughts were: *Will the answers come to me in the morning? If they don't, I may lose my mind.*

185

Chapter 19

Deputy Roccini was exhausted but she drove home, changed into a clean uniform and had a glass of orange juice and a reheated pancake for breakfast. Still wired from the wreck and all that went on earlier in the morning caused things to swirl around in her brain--the stone, the drenching rain, the phone call from Tippiny. Was there a link tying them all together? Mojo? No answers. She put it out of her mind and drove to the station intending to take another look at the old records on Goldie's case if she could find them amidst the clutter on Hunter's desk.

She wasn't surprised to find Hunter's car in his parking spot and him already sitting at his desk drinking a cup of coffee. She walked in and plopped in the chair in front of him. "You couldn't sleep, either, right?" She noticed he had changed clothes since the last she saw him, but flecks of mud were still stuck in his hair. He must not have had time for a shower.

"Nope. Wouldn't have gotten more than an hour or so." He pulled on his shirt. "I ran home to put on a fresh uniform and came on in." He pulled a paper out of his pocket. "Surprise! I stopped by Judge Taylor and got a warrant to search Mama Cheche's premises."

Zita patted her pants. "Great! I made a quick trip home, too. Needed to get refreshed after standing in the rain dealing with Mama."

Hunter gave her a wink. "No problem. You look and smell much better than I do right now. Okay, so what's the skinny on that stone and Mama Cheche?"

Yawning, she poured a cup of coffee for herself. "I couldn't wait to tell you, if I can stay awake long enough. Here goes: Mama Cheche has a stone she has kept in her mojo bag." She made a circle with her thumbs and forefingers. "It's a plain old brown rock about three inches in diameter, rounded on the top, but shiny. It has a 'D' on the flat side. Grandma Dee, her grandmother, just gave it to her. Ties in with the mojo she's always claimed to have. I think Mama expects it to solve our mystery about Goldie and who killed him."

The sheriff's head bobbed up and down. "Um-hum. It might be foolishness to me and you but to her it's as real as the sun rising every morning. Of course, I wouldn't turn down any help in solving this crime as long as it's legit."

Zita's back stiffened. "When we go back, you might get some from an unexpected source soon." She leaned forward. "Here's another tidbit. While I was there Tippiny, her daughter who's a lawyer, called." She gave him all the details, ending with, "We may have the case solved by the time this female attorney gets here."

"Mama Cheche keeps surprising me! Her daughter is a lawyer? We need to find out what we can do about this woman. We also might learn something if we can just get Mama to open up. She knows lots more than she's telling." He was up and pacing back and forth at this point, then he stopped and slapped his leg. "I've got an idea! If you can get your bones to move, let's go visit Mama again, we can catch her while she's tired and maybe off guard. We'll play a little game with her and pretend we go for the mojo magic. She likes doughnuts; we'll pick up some to 'sweeten' her up a bit."

Zita brightened up. "You know what, Boss? Your plan sounds thin, but it just might work." Eyes wide open and rejuvenated, she followed the sheriff out the door. As they pulled up to the doughnut shop, Zita slapped her hand against her cheek. "I'm so tired I forgot one thing. The hole. On Mama's porch I stepped on a piece of dried putty.When I looked up, I saw it came from the ceiling. I couldn't get up there to inspect it, but it was the exact shape a bullet would make."

"What did Mama say about it?"

"Acted like she didn't know what I was talking about. I'll try again when we go back to check on her."

"Might be the best idea. We don't want to put Mama on the defensive. She's a stubborn old woman and she's got her ways, like the mojo. We have to respect them or she'll never tell us anything."

Fifteen minutes later, they were once more in front of Mama Cheche's row house, armed with a dozen donuts. Mama opened the door just as Zita made a fist to knock. They entered and saw three mugs and small plates on the table. One mug had coffee in it. Without asking, Mama poured hot coffee into the other two mugs. "I knew you were coming," she announced.

Shaking his head, Hunter placed the box of doughnuts in the center of the table and opened it. "Take your pick, Mama," he said.

Mama chose a chocolate coated one with peanuts on top. Saying, "My favorite," she took a bite followed by a sip of coffee and then laid the doughnut on her plate. Pulling out a tissue, she sneezed into it.

"Are you okay, Mama? You got awfully wet last night. I hope you didn't catch a cold." Zita squinted at her.

"Don't worry about me. I've been through lots of storms. Some not physical but life shaking. I weathered them all." She ate the rest of her doughnut and reached for a lemon puff. "These are mighty good. I haven't had any doughnuts, or lemon puffs, in a long time."

Hunter refilled his cup from the percolator. *Time to get down to business. But where to start?* He took a swig of coffee and then a deep breath. "Glad you're enjoying them. Look, Mama," he sat in the chair next to hers, covered her hand with his own, and leaned in to meet her eyes. She met his gaze and didn't snatch her hand back. "We need a little help. You knew we were coming and put out these cups." He didn't mention that Zita had said she'd be there this morning. "You've convinced me you've got the mojo. How about using it for a good cause?" She raised her eyebrows, but he didn't react or give her a chance to reply. "Look, we found those bones and they could be Goldie's. I have my doubts, but I think you believe they are. But why?" He removed his hand, leaned back, and folded his arms.

Mama didn't say a word, but Hunter hoped she realized it was time to start revealing a few things. She got up from her chair, walked into the bedroom, and returned with two books. One was a tattered Bible. She pointed to the other one, a Harvard Classic. "Miss Eleanor Tollar," she paused, "er, Parsons, gave Mama and me a whole set of those when she left Cleveland. I used them to learn to read and to educate myself since there wasn't much here for a black girl. I may not be the smartest person in the world, but I learned a lot that's helped me through the years. I don't let anyone keep me down. It rubbed off on Tippiny."

She opened the book. "There's a story in this volume that reminds me of Robert Johnson, the famous blues singer everybody says went to the Crossroads and sold his soul to the devil. That's what Dr. Faustus did. People in Cleveland wondered if Wylie Martin turned out the same way--got greedy and wanted the whole world, like Dr. Faustus and," she tapped the Bible, "Some said Wylie might have been jealous of Goldie Parsons catching up with his fame and he got so afraid of losing money because of it that he killed Goldie." She leaned close to Hunter and asked, "Now what do you think of that, Sheriff?"

She's turning the tables on me. Does she think Goldie was murdered? How does she know? Hunter leaned his chin on his balled-up fist. "It's a possibility, Mama, but do you have anything to prove it?"

Mama placed the worn Bible on the table and then laid her hand on its cover. "I know they had an argument a couple of days before Goldie went missing. I'll swear on the Bible right here to that."

Zita didn't speak but she cut her eyes in Hunter's direction.

"That wouldn't help." *She's putting me on. I'll try another tack.* "Rocconi thinks that is a bullet hole in your porch ceiling. How did it get there, Mama? Did it have anything to do with Goldie?"

Mama's eye twitched. "Er, it's been so long ago, I don't remember." She snapped her fingers. "Maybe it was when someone shot at those foxes that hung around stealing chickens." Her hand touched the corner of the Bible. "On second thought, something did happen one night about the time Goldie went missing. Sheriff, I can't tell you anymore now. But the time is coming soon. I know I've got things to get off my conscience before I die. I am an old woman."

She picked up the stone that was on the table and turned to Hunter.

"I've learned a little more. A new development makes this complex. Your deputy can tell you I found out there may be a descendant. Goldie may have a granddaughter. Tippiny wants me to talk to this woman who says her grandma called her Goldie, and I should do that first before making any statements." Her voice shook.

She looked at Zita. "Tippiny insisted that I have to talk to this woman. You heard her on the phone. This could affect Tippiny's career."

She rubbed the top of the stone and held it out to Hunter. "Put your hand on this." When he looked wary, she added, "Humor me. Go ahead, it won't hurt you.

Hunter touched the smooth top of the stone.

"See," Mama said. "Nothing happened. But it has the power and it speaks to me. Sheriff, I can't say anymore. It's not time yet. For my daughter's sake, I have to wait."

Hunter sighed. "Mama, you're as stubborn as they come. Why don't you give me a hint about what you know and I'll try to follow through."

Mama blankly stared into space, swaying side to side. As if in a trance, she hummed the tune *Feelin' Reelin'*. "The levee did rise and cough up those bones," she said in a ghostly voice. She blinked back to reality. "That's all I'm going to say, Sheriff."

"What about the hole, Mama?"

She shook her head and stood. "I need to leave now. I'm going back to check those bones," she said in dismissal.

Convinced that's all they were going to get from Mama today, Hunter motioned to Zita and they left. In the car, he told her. "I'm going to drive around behind the row houses and give Mama time to leave. Maybe I won't need to upset her by pulling out the warrant. We'll go back and dig out that bullet if one's still there. I saw a ladder around the side of the house." He chuckled. "Looks like it's been there for years. I'll use it."

Before they drove off, Mama passed by carrying her willow stick. Zita turned to Harley. "You know, I don't think Mama even needs that stick. She's pretty steady on her feet. She probably carries it for a weapon to ward off dogs, or maybe intruders like us." Her lilting laugh lightened Hunter's mood. It was a refreshing moment in a serious situation. Zita was an attractive gal, equally important, she was super smart. Maybe at some point...*No, I can't go there. This relationship has to stay professional for it to work.*

As he maneuvered the car around the back, he refocused. "Yep, I'm sure she considers us intruders, or worse. That's why I didn't want to probe around on her porch with her there. Couldn't be so lax in Texas. Big city rules have to be followed. Cleveland's more like Mayberry." He pulled the car to a stop, waited a few minutes, and then hopped out. "Okay, Deputy, Mama's out of sight now. Let's get this done before she gets back and tells us we need a warrant. Wouldn't put it past her to threaten us with that stick."

Harley grabbed the ladder and brought it up on the porch, glad it had been easily accessible. These old row houses were built tall, so despite his height, he had to climb to the top rung to reach the spot. Harley used his pocket knife to pick at the putty that still remained and after pulling off a few chunks, what he sought plopped into his hand. Somehow the bullet that caused the hole was still lodged in the tin. He shook with excitement as the bullet fell from his hand to the porch floor. "Bingo!" he called out as he descended the ladder. Zita picked it up with a handkerchief and studied it in the palm of her hand. "This is from a .38 revolver. Man, you reckon it's been there sixty years?" She handed it to Harley.

"Hard to believe, but I don't doubt it." He looked down the road. Mama was walking as fast as she could in their direction. "Get ready, Rocconi. Mama's coming back. Doesn't really matter. We need to confront her."

When Mama reached hearing distance, she called out, "What are you doing? Maybe it's a good thing I forgot my phone."

It's best to be up front. "We needed to check out that hole in the porch ceiling, Mama. I didn't think you'd mind."

She poked a fist on one hip. "Well, I do. Just what did you find?"

Harley held out his hand, opened it, and showed Mama the bullet in his palm. "Know anything about this?" His eyes locked with hers.

Mama's eyes rolled and she leaned backward. Zita caught her and got her to an old rocking chair, the only piece of furniture on the porch. Sitting there leaning forward she mumbled unintelligible words that sounded like "Zoo, shoo--ing, badam, blues man, Gramma."

"Are you all right, Mama? What are you saying?" Zita asked.

Reaching for her head, Mama patted a spot above her right ear. "Ooh, it hurts. I couldn't think straight. Behind the tree. Dizzy. A man; a guitar. Gone, all gone." Her eyes were still rolling. She shook her head and her eyes snapped back to focus on Zita standing over her.

"I'm all right." She stood using her stick. When Zita tried to help her, she shoved her arm aside. "I said I'm all right."

"Okay, then," Hunter spoke up. "When did all this happen? Tell us about this. Did it hit you?"

She tapped the ground with her stick. "In - due - time." Mama emphasized each word. "Don't threaten to take me to the station, Sheriff. I know, and you know, you don't have enough evidence to keep me long. Look, let me tell you one more time--look at the song. I keep getting vibes about it and I believe the answer's in it. Before you ask, no, I haven't found it myself." She ambled toward the front door. "That's all I'm going to say. You may as well be on your way."

Hunter knew when he'd been defeated. He put the ladder back on the side of the house. The bullet in the twisted handkerchief went into his pocket. He turned to Zita. "Damn! Mama's acting like she had another vision. Mojo again. You notice she ended with the rhymed couplet? I say it's acting. How the hell are we going to dig anything out of that old woman?"

After driving back to the station and making sure Chan was there to take care of the office, he and Zita needed to get some rest. They were too tired to figure this out now. "We need to go home and take a nap," Hunter told his deputy. "I'm beat. That's what I'm going to do."

As she got into the patrol car he called out, "Relax and put this case out of your mind for now. "

Hunter slammed his fist against the steering wheel. *Yeah, like that's possible.*

Chapter 20

Attempting to get some sleep, Hunter tossed and turned in bed and flipped through that folder in his mind. The photos of the bones flashed by first. He visualized the body parts, the holes made by the two bullets, one that hit the chest, and then the other that went through the skull. How could either of those have reached Mama's porch ceiling? The bones were not of a giant. He racked his brain. *What were those words Mama mumbled? One was 'badam'. Could that be 'bad aim'? Maybe a killer who'd never used a gun before? Is there anything in the song about that?*

Hunter reached for the laptop he'd brought with him from Texas, one he'd bought hoping research at home would help him find that serial child killer. He sat up in bed and accessed the song. After printing it, he studied the words line by line. He pulled out a pencil and circled the lines, *It won't be long, before I'm gone,* it struck him how true they were. Next, he circled *Eventually, Levees' floods redeem me, I got a feelin', It got me reelin'* and *I'm tellin' you, Right here's the clues.* Drawing a thin line, he connected the two phrases.

199

After tossing the pencil across the room, balling up the paper, and sending it soaring as well, he cried out, "Damn it to Hell! If those clues are there why can't I find them? How else can I do what the song says and *Let justice come, For this wronged son?* He got up, picked up the paper off the hardwood floor, smoothed it, and gritted his teeth. "I'm not giving up."

Hunter checked the first words of lines again, but nothing fit together. He also tried pairing words at the ends of lines; that didn't produce any results either. After various efforts to find a pattern, he saw none. No clues about "aim" were in the song. At one point, something about letters tried to form in his mind, but it wouldn't work. It was late and he was too tired to make his brain function.

Slamming the computer shut, Harley tossed it onto the empty side of his bed. *Gotta get some sleep, but not much. I need a clear head to process this. I sure can't wait on Mama and her daughter. I've got less than a year as sheriff here; I've got to figure this out myself. Hell, Mama may never come through with any information anyway.* He stared at the song lyrics again. *I'd be in better shape if I believed in the mojo.*

Two hours later, Hunter awakened with a jolt, the alarm clock flashing three a.m. In his mind's eye, he had his hand on Mama's stone. Recalling his dream, he found himself at the scene of the crime he'd been investigating. Goldie stood at the steps of Mama Cheche's porch dressed in a Zoot suit like the image he had of the blues singer. It was too dark for him to see anyone else, but he saw the flash of gunshots followed by the sharp blast they made when triggered.The first missed its mark, whizzing past his head into the darkness. The second was followed by a thud as it entered Goldie's chest and the third made a sickening noise as it burrowed into the singer's skull. The lyrics of *Reelin' Feelin'* drowned out the weak cries of a child. *Who was the child?* The music stopped and two people, dressed in white, rose out of the darkness and walked together. One was Goldie, his red hair standing out; the other, a much older woman dragging him along. A guitar Goldie was holding relaxed from his grasp and fell to the ground. A shadowy figure, indistinguishable as a male or female in the darkness, picked it up and darted into the woods behind the row houses.

Oh, my God! I touched the stone! That dream. Damned if it doesn't seem like the mojo. But I don't believe in that stuff. It was just a nightmare--wasn't it? I already knew those things; they just resurfaced after I chewed on them before going to sleep. But he had to admit to himself that the dream provided more details than those that dwelled in his self-consciousness. It was much more vivid than words on paper. It was convincing. The name on that folder would most likely stay put.

Hunter tried to get back to sleep, but he was too worked up after the dream. He got up and took a long shower to try to wash away the mojo thoughts. All the way to the office, he rehashed the dream in his mind. No matter what, he'd have to tell Zita about it. Mojo or Nojo, it could lead to new clues, maybe a revelation.

***

Although a new problem surfaced--a tornado watch was in effect--it wasn't possible for Hunter to quit thinking about the case he dubbed the *Goldie Parsons' Case*. He'd even made a folder with that name, but only Zita had seen it. She'd laughed, asking, "What if these turn out not to be Goldie's remains?"

"I reckon we'll relabel the folder."

Later that morning, Zita sat in Hunter's office, across from his desk, mouth agape as Hunter retold his dream. "I don't know what to make of it." She shook her head. "I have mixed emotions about the mojo, but that is weird, especially the part about the man and the guitar. Mama hasn't mentioned anything like that. Where'd it come from?"

The phone rang. He smiled as he listened to the person on the other end. When he hung up, he snapped his fingers. "That was a ballistics' report. Sure enough, the bullet from Mama's porch came from that .38 revolver that we found here in the police station." He scratched his head. "Rocconi, didn't you say Mama Cheche found some bullets and a sales slip for them in the Tollar's house when she cleaned it after Mrs. Tollar died?"

"That's what she told me."

The conversation was interrupted when an unknown number flashed across his desk phone, "I wonder who this is?" He was in shock when he realized the call came from Mama Cheche. Her words were quick and he never got the chance to reply before she disconnected it. He put the receiver back on the hook and let out his breath. He told Zita, "That was Mama Cheche. She said to come out there. She's got something to show us. You'll never guess what it is."

Zita folded her arms. "Not a gun, is it?""

"Nope. A guitar. And Mama's opening up. She said she'll tell us the story about it." He put on his hat and headed for the door. "Tornado threat or not; we gotta go. Besides, we need to check to be sure Mama's safe. We'll make it quick."

Zita followed right on his heels, saying, "It's been a long wait, but this ought to be good."

***

To make sure Hunter got the guitar in case something happened to her, Mama called him to come to her house. She'd rush him out before Rita arrived. After stashing her packed suitcase in the bedroom, Mama met Hunter and Zita at the door with the guitar in hand. She explained how she'd acquired it without revealing how it came to be in Eli's possession. Despite them not being invited into the house, Hunter related that scene from his dream, but he told it as if he'd learned it in real life.

"How'd you know that? I was the only one, er…" she caught herself. "All I know is that I'm sure this was Goldie's guitar. That's all I'm going to share. I shouldn't even have called you."

Hunter opened his mouth, but she held up a palm. "Here," she handed him the guitar. "See if this can help you in any way. But," she shook a finger at him, "I want it back. If it was Goldie's, it'd be valuable." She sucked in her cheek. "Might be worth enough to pay for my funeral."

"Aw, Mama," Zita said, "you're not ready for that now. Not a spunky woman like you."

Mama grinned. "I plan to live till this case is solved." She waved them off. "Now take that guitar and leave me alone. "I've given you a couple of things, so keep me in the loop."

"Thanks, Mama, we will." She pointed to the sky."You know a tornado watch is up. Can you hear the wind picking up? Why don't you come with us?"

She lifted one shoulder. "No, I'll stay here. I've lived through a couple of those."

Zita made one more stab. "Okay, you're sure you don't have anything else to say?"

Mama sighed. "You're wasting your time. Go ahead and make it back to town before the weather gets worse."

They'd gotten a tidbit. No need to pressure her; she'd said as much as she was going to for now, so he and Zita left. As they drove away, Hunter clicked his tongue. "This weather is not looking good. Look at the wind kick up dust across these cotton fields. But we made a little progress. You made some brownie points with your last remarks, Deputy. Good job. Even if she wouldn't come with us, we've loosened Mama up. The curtain may be drawn for today, but just on act one. The show goes on. It isn't over, no, not by a long shot." *Next comes the song. Now all we have to do is find the clue.* His eyebrows formed a "V". *Damn! I'm picking up on Mama's rhymed couplets. Mojo, or what?*

Mary S. Palmer & Paula Lenor Webb

Chapter 21

On Hunter's drive back to the station, fear struck him when the sky turned a deep shade of green and the rain bore down so hard the windshield wipers couldn't keep up with it. He peered out the car's windows but the rain falling in torrential sheets, whipping the wind around the car prevented his seeing beyond a couple of feet. "Uh, oh. We're in for it. I can't see it, but I think a tornado is headed our way."

Zita scowled. "I can't see anything either. This is scary, Hunter." She touched his arm. "Looks like you're right."

"Yep. I'm from Texas and I know the signs. Everything is turning green; it's close." He pressed the accelerator to the floor. "We better get to shelter soon before we hear the sound of a steam engine roaring." He reached the Crossroads--the same Crossroads where many a bluesman sold his soul to the devil--and made a right turn toward Cleveland.

Hunter's heart sank as he heard the sound of a freight train near the patrol car. "Where is it? I can't see it in this driving rain. Can you see anything?"

"No, I can't!" she said as she looked in all directions.

Hunter slammed on the brakes when the trunk of a large oak tree landed inches away from the hood of the car. He shifted into reverse, with no other way of escape, but churned up ground filled with mud and its wheels sank deeper into the mud and muck. He glanced towards Zita, who had unbuckled her seat belt and curled into a tight ball on the floor of the passenger side. She was using her arms to protect her head. Feeling the car rock and the sound of the tornado even closer, he threw his body over hers to protect her from what was about to come. *Dear Lord, don't let us die here,* he thought as seconds felt like minutes.

Hunter got on his radio and asked for help knowing it was an act of futility. Nobody could reach them and get them out in time should the tornado take the path in their direction. He beat a fist into his other hand. What to do? *Why in the hell did I try to take a shortcut? I'd have been better off, maybe even back to the station by now if I'd stayed on the main road.*

Hunter raised his head an inch and looked at Zita. For the first time since he'd known her, she looked pale, and vulnerable. He lingered a moment. Feeling her body trembling under his, the instinct to shield her from danger became intense. It took all the willpower he could muster to move off of her. She wasn't his girlfriend; she was his deputy. But what could he do? No need to stress the seriousness of the situation; she knew that. "Climb into the back seat and get down on the floorboard," he said in a raspy voice. "I'll stay up front and keep an eye out. If you know any prayers, I'd suggest you say them."

The minute they were both in place, Hunter heard the roar. *Dear God, if it hits us, let it be me. Please protect Zita. This is my fault. Don't let her die.*

The sound came very close, then it moved away. For a few minutes, neither Hunter or Zita rose up. Then they both did so at the same time and faced each other. Zita laughed and so did Hunter. "We made it," she said. "God answered my prayers."

As quickly as the tornado arrived, it disappeared. The rocking ceased, the wind stilled, and the booming sound dissipated.

"I can't believe it! Now you see it, and now you don't. It's all over," Zita commented.

"Right." Hunter tried to see through the mud caked on the windows. Zita crawled out from the floorboard and stared at the windshield covered with mud. Mumbling curse words under his breath, Hunter got out of the car and surveyed the situation. Both back tires had sunk into the mud so deep only towing was going to get them out.

A siren blared out and he spotted a tow truck a few yards away. "Hey!" he called out. "Help has arrived." Hunter exited the car and waved his arms, signaling to the truck. "We're okay," he said when the driver got out and hooked up to the patrol car.

The grizzly truck driver replied in a husky voice that matched his frame, "You barely did. Look over yonder at that farmhouse, or what's left of it."

"That's the Winkler's house," Hunter said. "Man, it and the barn are a shambles. They're boths flattened on the ground like tiddlywinks. God, I hope nobody was in it."

"Naw, we already found out nobody was home. Damn good luck. Better than those folks had in that wreck on the Highway the other night." The driver got into his truck and pulled out the patrol car. He got back out, gathered his ropes, threw them into his truck bed, and then he got back into his truck and waved to Hunter. "You're good to go now. If I wuz you, I'd stay offa these back roads."

Hunter and Zita were both back in the front seat when he turned the car around and headed back to where he'd left the main highway. When they reached the Crossroads and took a left turn back towards the main road, they were in for another surprise. The tornado had skipped through the area, taking off roofs of one house and missing the one next to it. Some of the asphalt on the highway was also damaged. Hunter and Zita stared at each other. "Damnation! If we'd stayed on this road..." Hunter didn't finish the sentence. He guided the car down the cracked asphalt with his brain spinning. *Was it God's grace, fate, or Mama's mojo that saved them?* He sucked in his breath convinced he and his deputy were left on earth because they still had something to do here. And he knew exactly what it was.

Without an explanation, Hunter turned the car in the direction opposite from the route to the station.

"Where are you going?" Zita asked.

"Back to check on Mama. Her house isn't far from the one trashed."

When they got close, Zita saw extensive damage to the row houses--some were moved from their sills, others had rooms removed and dropped across the street. But she was relieved to see the tornado had skipped Mama's--almost. "Oh, look, Hunter," she exclaimed. "Mama's front porch is gone!"

Hunter pulled the patrol car as close as possible and got out. "Wait here. The floor may be rickety." He swung his body up onto the front door's threshold. "No need for both of us to take a risk." The wood cracked and his foot slipped through.

"You okay?" Zita asked.

"I'm fine." Hunter balanced by holding onto the door frame. Then he pulled his foot loose. Gingerly stepping into the living room he called out, "Mama, are you here? Are you okay?" No reply. Testing each board of the pine floor, he made his way through the house, opening the one closet's door and even looking under the bed in the bedroom. The bathroom was spotlessly clean, but empty. Nothing. Nobody home. He went to the back and found steps still in place. Then he looked under the house, aiming his flashlight in every corner. Sills were cracked and it looked like a couple shifted out of place, but no one had taken refuge there.

Hunter came around to the front shaking his head. "She's not here, Zita. I'm worried. I hope she wasn't on that porch when it was lifted into the air." He scanned the area. "You see anything that looks like Mama's porch?"Pointing to a spot down the road a piece, Zita pointed out something on top of a high pile of wreckage. "I think I see an arm of a rocking chair like the one that was on Mama's porch."

They walked over to the pile and Zita said, "Yep, this is Mama's chair all right. And I bet that stack of wood underneath it is her porch. Good Lord! This is unbelievable!"

Hunter pulled a few boards aside. Satisfied Mama wasn't buried underneath them, he looked down the road where a group of five men and women stood transfixed.

"Let's go ask them if they've seen Mama." He got on his phone and called for help.

When they reached the group, none of them spoke until one woman holding a crying baby said, "That was my house." She pointed to a large pile of debris. "I don't have any food for my baby."

"Help's on the way. They'll take all of you to safety and get food for your baby, Ma'am. We're looking for Mama Cheche. Have any of you seen her?"

The others shook their heads, but the woman said, "I, I saw her on her porch, not, not too long before, before this happened." Her voice shook as she stammered out the words. "Looked like she had a big old suitcase beside her. But I'm not sure."

Hunter looked into her vacant eyes. "How in the world did you get out?"

Squeezing the baby to her breast, the woman replied, "I don't know. I just found myself here after the, after, er, after everything was gone." She burst into tears.

Zita put her arm around the woman's shoulders. "It'll be alright." Then she directed her question to the entire group. "Was anyone else in there?"

All of them shook their heads. Zita said, "Well, you've lost a lot but you are alive."

When a commandeered Delta State University Band Bus pulled up and loaded the people into it, Zita had to hold back tears. Only then did she think of her own home, Hunter's Pink Palace at the Shackem Up Inn, and the station in town. Did any, or all, of those buildings end up destroyed, or were they spared? She didn't mention the unnerving possibilities because they headed back to the station and one by one, good or bad, she'd soon find out the answers.

Hunter was pensive on the slow ride as they searched left and right for Mama Cheche. They found no sight of her, nor were other citizens outside. When they got close to the station, he slapped the steering wheel. "You know something? It just struck me that when I looked in Mama's closet, the hangers were pushed back and it looked like clothes were missing." He scratched his ear. "I wonder if that old woman took it upon herself to leave town. You reckon?"

"Could be. But where would she go? All she's got is her daughter and Tippiny's in D. C.; how could Mama get there?"

"Humph! That old biddy's flexible. Got a lot of fire in her still. She might try anything. Maybe she decided to go visit Tippiny. I'm heading for the bus station. Wouldn't put it past her to take a Greyhound to Memphis and then fly to D. C."

The ticket clerk at the bus station said Mama hadn't been there. Also, because of the tornado warning, the buses had suspended operation earlier in the day. That part of the search for Mama came to a dead end.

"No need to check airlines in Memphis," Hunter told Zita. "I don't know how in the hell she'd get there from here, except on Greyhound."

When he and Zita drove by her house and returned to the station, happy to find both intact, Hunter told Deputy Chan to go back to the row house area and see if he would have any luck looking for Mama. He also said, "Stop by the Shackem Up Inn and let me know if it's still standing. I hope so, but I don't have much to lose." He pulled on his uniform shirt collar. "I'm wearing my best clothes and boots. All I have that's valuable is my laptop." Still he was relieved when Chan phoned to say all was safe and sound.

At the end of the day, the destruction in the Cleveland area proved to be those few houses around the Tollar property. No deaths were reported and injuries were minor, leaving the big mystery about one person: What had happened to Mama Cheche?

Chapter 22

Focus remained on Mama's location. Hunter found out the people brought in had been placed with relatives or friends, so he sought them out and asked about Mama again after they'd calmed down. Nothing new. The one woman stuck to her story about seeing Mama on her porch. Nothing new came to light.

At six p.m., Deputy Chan returned to the station and plopped into a chair in the Sheriff's office. "I haven't found out a thing about Mama Cheche. No luck at all. Then I checked the stores in town. Nobody has seen that woman today." He curled his lip. "You sure she still exists, Sheriff?"

"Talked to her myself earlier. Rocconi was with me." He got up and looked out the window. "Darned if I can figure this out. Can't believe she's a victim. They've sent crews out and gone through the destruction. Nobody there. If she was hurt, she'd have had to crawl away somehow and we can't find a trace of that." He pointed at the deputy. "Say, did you go down to the river?"

Chan nodded. "Checked every inch of that area, too. Where the bones were and up and down the entire section. Flood waters are higher than ever. But I didn't see a trace of anyone being around there. No footprints or anything. What do we do next, Boss?"

"Maybe we can get some dogs from Jackson. Time for me to check on the Parsons' case anyhow. See what they found out about the DNA of those bones, even though we have nothing to compare it to. Ha, with Mama disappearing we may never have any. Old Goldie's case could become colder than ever. He ran his hands through his hair. *Oh, God, no! That can't happen. I can't stand another failure.*

In the dead silence for a couple of minutes, Chan wriggled in his chair. "Well, Boss," he said, "you want me to call the folks in Jackson?"

Hunter shook off his trauma. "No, I'll have to do it myself to get results." He picked up the phone. "Damn it! Won't ring. Maybe their cell towers are down."

"I'm surprised our phones are working. Maybe theirs will clear up soon," Chan commented.

Hunter nodded. He hoped so, but things weren't going in his favor. He expected it would be tomorrow before he got a call through and longer before assistance came.

Chapter 23

It wasn't noon yet, but Mama's morning had been adventurous. For the first time in her life, she'd ridden down an Interstate Highway all the way to Memphis. She'd accepted rides from neighbors in Cleveland sometimes when it rained, but only to other small towns nearby or downtown. Most of the time, she walked wherever she went since she only cleaned houses close by. This time, that wasn't an option.

Other new things occurred, too. In one day, she'd ridden on that Interstate frightened for her life, they'd outrun a tornado, and now she awaited her first airplane ride. Her brain was spinning as she realized it was all real. Sitting in the Memphis Airport, watching the digital screen flash various destinations, she mused about all that had transpired.

Mama didn't tell Sheriff Harley and Zita about her phone call from Tippiny the night before. "Shannon Edwards can't come to Cleveland right now, but she really wants to meet you. She wants you to come here to meet her, Mama," her daughter announced. "I've made the arrangements for the plane trip from Memphis. The flight's at 3 p.m. tomorrow and…"

"Wait just a minute, Tippiny. I've never been on a plane in my eight decades on Earth, and I don't intend to…"

"Mama," Tippiny's tone was harsh, "This is a wonderful opportunity for a great experience. I will take care of all the expenses, Mama, you just have to get to the airport in Memphis. You will have so much fun! I'll give you a personal tour of Washington, D. C. and we can spend the day together. I have a bus ticket waiting for you at the Greyhound station for the trip to Memphis."

"Tippiny, listen to me. I'd love to see you and be with you. It's been so long since we've been together, but I'm too old and too set in my ways to go flying off and traipsing around big city streets. And you know I've never even ridden a Greyhound bus, either. I wouldn't…"

"Mama," Tippiny's voice became louder and more forceful. "You listen to me. I'm here for three more days. This is my one chance to make a good impression on Shannon. You know Congressman Waters, the man you see on the TV all the time? She is his personal attorney! If we do this right, she can get me some great connections. It could mean I'd end up a constitutional attorney for congressmen. And this depends a lot on you!"

"Baby, I just can't…" her voice cracked. She wanted the best for Tippiny, but this was so much.

"Mama," Tippiny blurted out in a throaty voice, "do you ever want to see me again?"

She pushed the right button. Mama never could deny her daughter anything for long. And life without her only child would be unlivable. Weakening, she justified her change of heart. This was an opportunity of a lifetime, a way to learn about history, to see the White House, the Pentagon, the Washington Monument, which she'd only seen on her calendar, and maybe the Smithsonian. Places she'd read about in a National Geographic magazine in a doctor's office, places she'd never imagined touring. She sighed. *I give in too easily. But Tippiny's all I've got. This might be my last chance to spend any time with her.*

"All right, Tippiny," Mama conceded, "you win."

"Wonderful!" She made kissing noises. "I'll meet you at the airport late tomorrow. I love you. Bye."

Mama had wanted to say, "Really?" but she didn't. No need to cloud the issue. Instead, she went to her closet and pulled out a water-stained cardboard suitcase someone had left in one of the houses she cleaned out, packing it with her best clothes. Ambling into the bathroom, she got her toothbrush and hair brush. If she needed anything else for those few days in D. C., Tippiny could take her to the store.

She saved her best church dress, a green one with yellow butterflies flying all over it, for the plane trip. On the foot of the bed, she laid the dress and a jacket with large pockets. She also stuffed a pair of stockings in her Sunday shoes, and placed them beside the bed. After she double-checked the contents of her suitcase, she closed it and tied a piece of twine around the base to hold it together. And she put her willow stick on top. *Tippiny said she plans on sightseeing. If we do much of it, I'm going to need my stick. I just hope I can get around enough to see some of those famous places.*

Mama never carried a purse, she didn't need to. Her Grandma Dee showed her how to sew pockets into her clothes when she was a little girl and they still served a purpose. She used a large black bag shoved to the back of the closet shelf to store her *mad money.* If this didn't fit the moment, nothing did. She had saved it for a special occasion. Excitement intensified: This was it.

She pulled her older dresses aside and reached for the bag, dragging it forward. It slipped from her grip and fell on the floor at her feet. Picking it up, she unzipped the top and counted the money inside--enough for unknown expenses, and a couple of cheap meals, with an extra two-hundred in case her heart acted up or there was some other emergency. Tippiny would take care of anything she could not think of and she told her most of the museums in D. C. were free.

Not willing to travel far without her mojo bag, Mama placed it and the cash into her zippered jacket pocket. She glanced at the jacket's worn-edged sleeves and a stitched rip on one side and laughed. *I'll be in style.*

Mama recalled rising at six a.m. and listening to the local blues radio station as she watched the sun slowly rise from her porch while sipping her coffee. It surprised her to hear on the radio that bad weather was headed their way. She just finished her last sip when the phone rang; it was Tippiny. "Mama, I got a text from Greyhound. There is a weather alert and buses have stopped running for the morning. We need a way to get you to Memphis in time to catch that flight. I'll hire a cab from Memphis to drive down and pick you up. I'll call you back."

Tippiny hung up before Cheche could reply. Mama paced around the room. She didn't want to ride in a cab for over a hundred miles with a stranger. *Dear God, what...Wait a minute. At church Sunday, I think the preacher's aunt said her visit was coming to an end and she'd be driving back to Memphis today.* She called Tippiny back. "Don't hire a cab, Tippiny. I have a better idea." She told Tippiny about the preacher's aunt and gave her the preacher's phone number to contact the woman.

"Good, I'll call him and ask to speak to her. I can wire them some money. I'll give them a good donation to make it worth their efforts. I'll call you right back."

"Now I don't want anybody to know about this," Mama said. "You figure out how to keep it a secret."

Ten minutes later, Tippiny called back. "The preacher's aunt answered his phone, amazing isn't it? I asked her, 'Would you like some company today on your trip home and a little extra cash in your pocket?' Her name is Rita, by the way. She replied, 'Yes, I would, especially with bad weather expected, but you just caught me. I'm leaving in ten minutes. Can she be ready?'"

Tippiny chuckled. "I told her you're ready now and gave her your street address. She refused any money. I told her that your trip is a surprise. She said she wouldn't have anyone to tell about it anyhow. So your secret's safe."

Mama blinked, she realized she was in the Memphis Airport. Life was real and she'd soon be on her way to the nation's capital. Business had been taken care of. She was glad she'd given that guitar to the sheriff and she was proud that she'd gotten rid of him and Zita before Rita arrived to take her away.

Hopefully this trip provided new information. If her suspicions were correct and Shannon was Goldie Parsons granddaughter then maybe, just maybe, hidden facts would come to light. She glanced around the airport seeing people rushing everywhere. She also noticed empty seats in the waiting area and realized how lonely she was. It was sad to feel so alone in a room packed with people. But most were on cell phones or reading books and magazines. She took out her phone to see if Tippiny had called. She had not. But Mama did see a new number, from Dallas, Texas, and the caller had left a message.

She stared at the phone. *Who in the world is calling me from Texas? Is this the Sheriff? Did he figure out I left?*

She listened to the message and heard an unfamiliar voice, "Ms. Cheche, my name is Jenny Stein and I'd like to ask you a few questions. Please call me. It's about the Goldie Parsons case." No other explanation was given.

Mama shrugged. "Curious, but I'm not going to fool with that now. Maybe I'll call back when I return home." She put the phone into her pocket, letting her thoughts drift back to the eventful trip to Memphis.

It was twenty minutes before Rita flew down her driveway in a Cadillac, the fanciest car Mama had ever ridden in. Nothing like the pick-up trucks of neighbors who gave her rides. As they headed for the Interstate, irritated at Rita's delay ,Mama didn't feel like talking. "So sorry," she faked a whisper. "I got a sore throat. If I talk, it gets worse."

Rita, a chatterbox, didn't appear to mind. She made continuous conversation while Mama listened, nodding now and then. That was adequate. Much of Rita's idle rambling centered on the weather and didn't require a response.

When they reached the Interstate on the longest stretch of the trip, they noticed the clouds in the distance and how dark they became the closer they got. The Memphis station's radio announcer said a Tornado Warning was now in effect, and the pitch blackness, rain and wind that now surrounded them confirmed it. Rita said, "Look for a sign saying where the next exit is. We can't keep driving in this."

A mile down the road Mama told her driver, "There's a sign. The next exit is nineteen miles."

Rita mumbled an expletive as the rain came down harder and the wind shook the car. She checked her rear view mirror and turned white. "We'll have to speed up," she said with the car jerking forward as she pressed the gas pedal.

Mama stiffened and tightened her seat belt as she saw the speedometer rise to eighty and then to ninety, rain blinding her view of the road. She saw Rita gripping the steering wheel to keep the car on the road. Even in this weather, a sport's car raced by them. Other cars also passed them by. What was behind them? She was afraid to look. Powerful, whipping wind made the car sway a bit from side to side, adding further risk. Fear, not a faked sore throat, made Mama speechless. All she could think of was reaching that exit and how much longer it would take to get to Memphis, so she could get out of this vehicle. She was more concerned about the danger in the car than of the tornado close on their heels outside.

For a few miles, neither woman spoke. Rita kept checking her rear view mirror and struggling to keep the car on the road in the blinding wind and rain. "I bet it's coming our way," she said. She added pressure to the gas pedal and Mama shook as the speedometer edged its way past a hundred. She felt as if she were already flying before she got in a plane. She mouthed prayers as she stared straight ahead. She knew this wasn't where she was destined to die, but it was so frightening it made her wonder if the mojo was wrong. Maybe she'd never get to see her daughter again. What a way to go!

Traveling at such a high rate of speed, Rita couldn't slow down fast enough to make the turn on the exit for North Tunica. She muttered, "Damn," and kept moving. A few miles later, the wind and rain subsided by the time they reached the next exit, the one where the floating casinos parked along the Mississippi River. Then Mama saw the number on the speedometer drop until it reached the seventy-five mile per hour speed limit. Rita relaxed her grip on the steering wheel and shook her head. "We outran the tornado. I can't believe it! I think I saw it dip down in the distance. God is good!" She took one hand off the steering wheel and pointed to the left. "Over there."

They turned right after they saw a road sign directing them to the Memphis International Airport and Graceland. Mama was relieved. Her number wasn't up yet. She was more relieved when Rita dropped her off at the entrance to the airport.

"Don't we have a story to tell!" Rita said to Mama as she pulled her suitcase out of the trunk, placed it on the curb, and handed her the walking stick. "I will give you a call the next time I'm in Cleveland." Mama nodded and waved as Rita drove out of sight.

As Mama surveyed the area, an observant porter introduced himself, picked up her bag, helped her check in, got her boarding pass, and offered to find her flight..

"Why thank you, young man," Mama replied. This time, she used her willow stick to help her along. Her rubbery legs would not have made it to the inside of the terminal. The porter asked, "Ma'am, it's a long way to your gate; would you like a cart to ride in?" She nodded as he made a call on his walkie talkie and another porter soon drove up on a cart. The young man got off to help her get into the passenger seat and then he hopped back into the driver seat.

He told her all about his own grandmother as he zipped through the airport. Mama sat there on the ride, grateful to find such a helpful person and trying to figure out how much tip she should give him, like she saw people do on TV--maybe two dollars. It was then that an oddity hit her: *Here I am going from one Delta to another. The Mississippi Delta to Delta Airlines. At least I made it this far. After a wild ride and a brush with a tornado, a plane ride should be a breeze. No matter what is next, I'm going to make it the rest of the way, God willing.*

While riding on the cart, her cell phone rang. "Mama, it's Tippiny. Are you at the airport? Is everything going alright?

Mama said, "Yes, Tippiny," and decided to wait to tell her about the wild ride later. "This nice young man is carting me to my plane now."

"Okay. Be sure to keep your cell phone with you. If it needs charging, they have stations in the waiting area. I'll keep in touch and call you when your plane lands about going to Baggage Claim."

The porter rolled her to the proper gate. She handed him two one-dollar bills and when he didn't thank her, she dug out an extra dollar and passed it to him; then, he smiled.

It had been a new experience, one Mama never expected to have. Now, she sat in the gate area in an uncomfortable chair staring at empty ones opposite her. She squinted at the departure board, studied it a minute, and figured out that it meant her plane would arrive on time. But she still had over an hour. Her stomach growled, so she went back to the concourse to get a bite to eat. Onions frying in the first restaurant she passed caught her attention. She looked at the posted menu above the counter. *Five dollars for a hamburger and three fifty for fries, plus, three dollars for iced tea and it may need sweetening.* Mama shook her head. *My money's not going to last long on this trip.* She ordered the hamburger and fries. She was surprised when they charged two-dollars for the bottled water she ordered to save money.

As she sat at a table to eat, she savored the tasty flavor of the ground beef. Maybe it was worth more than the ones they served at the Delta Diner in Cleveland. As she took the last bite of her meal, she glanced at a man leaving another table who left a five-dollar bill beside his empty paper plate with remnants of the same order she had. Mama cupped her chin in her hands. *Good Lord, am I going to make it to Washington, D. C. with any money left?* She pulled out one dollar and slipped it under the corner of her water bottle. *That man may be on an expense account, but I'm not. This is all I can afford.* She used her stick and hurried out of the restaurant as fast as she could move.

By the time she got back to the Delta gate, a crowd had gathered. Lines formed at the counter and most chairs were filled. She found an empty one and eased into it. The matronly lady with a hairdo to heaven seated next to her moved her elbow from the armrest between them and smiled. Then she turned back to texting on her cell phone. The heavy set man on the other side was absorbed in reading a magazine.

Mama sat there with her hands folded in her lap and nothing to do. Being alone in a crowd was worse than being alone in familiar woods. She was glad when they announced boarding started. She'd been told she could board with the first group, so she walked to the agent checking boarding passes. She took her time and used her stick going from the rotunda to the cabin. A stewardess welcomed her aboard and pointed out where she'd find her seat. Mama was glad to have a window seat so she could see the view. She'd fastened her seat belt and settled in when the husky man seated next to her at the gate stuffed a carry-on bag into the overhead compartment and squeezed into the seat next to her, stepping on Mama's toes. "Sorry," he grumbled.

"That's all right, Sir. My name is…" she held out her hand, but he looked away and didn't take it, so she didn't finish the sentence. He scrunched down in his seat, closed his eyes, and turned his head toward the male passenger on his other side. *So much for being friendly.* Mama raised the window shade as high as it would go and watched a man on a cart on the asphalt below moving luggage. She grimaced when she saw her own tossed into the belly of the plane. Then she watched the stewardess' body language instructions while watching the video of what to do when. Before she realized it, they were off the ground and ten thousand feet into the air.

Despite the tension of her first flight, with no one to talk to and nothing to read, Mama forced herself to fall asleep. When she awakened, she asked the stewardess when they'd be in D. C. and was surprised to find she'd slept through the stop in Atlanta and they'd soon be landing in Washington.

As the plane descended it shook slightly, causing Mama's body to tremble internally. Then her eyes started rolling, a sure signal that a vision was coming. One that nobody but her would know about. The "knowin' of what was comin'" was about to be revealed. She felt it in her bones.

Mama sat tense and rigid. Her body wasn't moving but it felt like her head was spinning in circles. Her stomach churned, too. She took a deep breath and waited for the vision to appear. Time moved backwards. She saw herself as a ten year-old girl in the dark by her front porch. Grandma Dee held her hand. Two men were struggling for control of a gun. It went off and a bullet whizzed past, scraping Cheche's forehead. She fell to the ground and saw the men close by her feet. The taller of the two pulled loose of a clutch hold and reached for a guitar that had fallen to the ground. A shot exploded and blood flowed from that man's head. Another shot hit him in the chest. He let out an earth-shaking scream that sounded like a screech-owl. After three attempts, he struggled to his feet and stood stock still. The other man picked up the guitar and threw the strap across his shoulder. With the gun in his hand and cackling like a madman, he turned and ran into the woods.

Grandma Dee's words reverberated in Mama's brain. "Honey chile," she said as she turned loose of her granddaughter's hand, "You go on back in the house." She swayed side to side. "My time has come and so has Goldie's. I'll help him along. We goin' down to the river."

She gave Cheche a peck on the cheek. "Now you remember the mojo. Use it right. Say yo' prayers to the Father, the Son, and the Holy Spirit and everythin' will be alright."

With Goldie in tow, Grandma Dee had disappeared into the darkness. Cheche didn't make any attempt to follow them or the man with the gun. She said a prayer and then did as she was told, slipping into the house and sneaking back in bed.

Mama leaned over and placed her face into cupped hands. The man next to her said, "Ma'am, are you okay? Didn't you hear the announcement? We've landed in Washington." He stood and pulled his bag down from the overhead bin. The man who had the aisle seat had already left. She was almost the last one on the plane."

Without replying, Mama got up, edged past the empty seat on her left, and stood in the aisle to deplane. Her legs were so shaky that even her stick couldn't completely steady her, but she moved at a slow pace. By the time she got to the jet bridge, she was walking much better. A flight attendant wished her farewell with a smile and Mama moved on.

Mama pulled her cell phone from her jacket pocket and noticed that Tippiny had called many times. She dialed Tippiny's number and assured her she had arrived. Tippiny was already waiting at the Baggage Claim. "Get a skycap and he'll bring you right here, Mama," Tippiny said.

Mama paused. "What is a skycap?"

She heard Tippiny sigh. "I'll tell you what. Baggage Claim isn't far. Just follow the sign and the crowd and you'll be here shortly."

But Mama couldn't keep up with the passengers hurrying on their way. So when she asked an attendant for a skycap, she flagged one down and she helped Mama into the ride. *Three more dollars gone. This is getting too expensive.* It became more expensive tip-wise because when they reached a turning point he turned her over to another porter with a cart. This time, when they reached Baggage Claim, Mama spotted Tippiny and motioned to her. "I only have a five dollar-bill," she whispered as she gave her daughter a hug. "Do you have a couple of ones?"

"No," Tippiny said in an abrupt tone while backing off. She looked around. "Baggage is coming. Just give him the five. It doesn't matter." She left. "I'll go get your luggage. What color is your bag?"

Mama replied, "It's brown, that old cardboard one." She handed the man the five dollars and asked for two dollars change.

He dug into his pocket and pulled out a dollar. "That's all the change I've got."

Tippiny headed in her direction with the bag hidden as best she could by her side. Mama shooed the porter   away.

"Mama," Tippiny blurted out, "why didn't you bring that satchel of yours? This bag's a disgrace. I'm ashamed to be seen carrying it."

Mama blinked back tears. "I'm sorry to embarrass you, Baby. Give it to me; I'll carry it." She couldn't contain a sob. So much change came so fast, she struggled to keep up.

Tippiny waved her off and put her arm around her mother's shoulders. "I'm sorry, Mama. I'm just tired. Forget I said that. How was your first flight on a plane?"

Mama smiled. "Not as bad as I thought. I slept through most of it." No need to tell her daughter about the vision, she'd have sloughed it off. She didn't believe in the mojo.

At the exit, sliding glass doors opened up when they got close and Mama said, "Those are just like the ones at the department store back home." Tippiny gave her a quick stare and went outside to hail a cab.

Mama was glad Tippiny was in charge of getting her around, people were everywhere! Tippiny led her to the terminal and to a cab queue where they waited until an attendant directed them to a cab. The driver hopped out and opened the passenger door for Mama. "Welcome to Washington, D. C.!"

"You get up front, Mama." Tippiny handed the driver Mama's bag to place in the trunk, slipped into the back seat, and told the man, "Potomac Restaurant."

"Tippiny, that sounds fancy. I am good with a burger. I want to see the Washington Monument. I missed seeing it through the plane window when we flew in. Let's go..."

Tippiny cut her off. "I texted Shannon while I was waiting for you. We're meeting her there and she has already reserved a table. You will love it! It's the finest restaurant in D. C. Seats about a thousand people and it has a gorgeous view of the Potomac. Offers all kinds of gourmet fare. Congressmen eat there and every now and then the President shows up. He has a secluded area and more security guards than you can count, so if he happens to be there, we will not get to see him. Anyway, you'll love it."

"Over a thousand people? I'll bet it's plenty pricey, too. I'd be fine with a burger. Look!" Mama saw the pointed top of what had to be the Washington Monument, the famous obelisk. "I still want to go..."

Tippiny acted like she didn't hear her mother. "Relax, Mama. I'm on an expense account. Even if I weren't, nothing's too good for my mother." She squeezed her mother's hand. "This is a chance for me to really show you a good time."

Mama didn't say so, but she wasn't so sure about all of this.

Twenty minutes of the cab zipping in and out of busy traffic, then it pulled to the restaurant entrance. Tippiny paid the fare with a credit card and helped Mama out of the car while the cabbie took her bag out of the trunk. Looking around to see if anyone noticed the beat up old suitcase, she tossed it into the back seat of the cab and said, "Mama, we can't carry this around. I'm going to send it to the hotel." She gave the driver a twenty dollar bill and a business card she pulled out of her purse. "Take this to the Arlington Arms Hotel and have them put it in my room." He nodded thanks.

"Your jacket's, er, rumpled. Take it off and give it to me," Tippiny said. Cheche kept her mouth shut, but she was not happy with the way Tippiny was treating her things, her bag and now her jacket, especially since her mojo bag and money were in it. But she did as she was told.

Tippiny rolled Mama's jacket into a ball and stuffed it into her large purse. Feeling chilly from the air off the river, and embarrassed by her simple attire, Mama looked at her plain dress and felt more out of place than she ever had in her life.

As they entered the restaurant through massive stained-glass doors, Mama slowed her pace, using the stick to help navigate the marble steps. The only place she had ever gone into that was even close to the size of this restaurant was the supermarket in Cleveland. She was about to venture into a realm of society the complete opposite of where she'd been all of her life. And she was going to meet a woman who ranked right up there with the President of the United States. Her knees shook so bad even her stick became unsteady. *This is all entirely foreign to me. How in the world will I fit in or even be able to communicate? I won't.*

Mary S. Palmer & Paula Lenor Webb

Chapter 24

The stiff-necked maitre d', dressed in a tuxedo and black tie, opened the massive doors and greeted them in the restaurant's foyer. Looking down his nose at Mama, he turned to address Tippiny. "Do you have reservations, Ma'am?"

Tippiny gave him her name. Then his tone became more friendly. "Oh, Miss Brown, Miss Edwards is waiting for you." He snapped his fingers and a tall, well-dressed waiter approached and stood at attention.

"Take these lovely ladies to Miss Edwards' table." He nodded. "Enjoy your dining experience."

Mama wasn't impressed. "Tippiny, this is a lot of fuss for a meal."

"Shhh, Mama! Enjoy it!"

They followed the waiter to the table with the best view of the Potomac River where Miss Edwards stood to greet them. "So, you're Mrs. Brown, Tippiny's mother."

She grasped both of Mama's hands and squeezed them. "How do you do? I've heard so much about you."

How could that be? She just met Tippiny. I'm not so sure about this one. Mama charged her remark up to big city ways. Picking up on the lead, she replied. "I have heard about you, too, and what an important job you have." She leaned forward. "And you're so pretty! My goodness, I haven't seen that shade of red hair in over fifty years. Goldie Parson's hair was that color. I'm too old and my time is too short to not be honest with you. I bet you are related to him, that light skin doesn't fool me. I see his blue eyes looking at me now. I'm happy to meet you." Mama could feel the mojo tingling through their locked hands.

From the corner of her eye, she noticed Tippiny's lip curl and realized she'd said the wrong thing. But what was the right thing? She didn't know. Shannon was speechless and Tippiny squirmed in her chair.

Mama sat down in the chair the waiter pulled out for her. He reached around in front of her, and she flinched when he dropped a large green napkin in her lap. It matched the table cloth, even with the small tree in the center. Mama took a deep breath. This was all new to her. She tried to lean her stick against the chair next to her, but it slipped and hit the marble floor with a thud. Even though tables were spaced a good distance apart, heads glanced her way as she tried to pick it up. Before she reached it, the waiter retrieved it and placed it sideways by her chair without saying a word.

Moving past the shock, Shannon lightened the mood by patting Mama's hand. Again, Mama felt the tingle of mojo and met her intense blue eyes. "Don't worry. No problem. Things like that happen," Shannon reassured her. "Now," she glanced at the wine menu and then put it aside. "Let's order some champagne while we decide on what we'll have for dinner." She turned to Mama. "You do like champagne, don't you?"

Mama thought of the old preacher man who tried to get her to drink his wine years ago. She didn't accept it then, nor had she imbibed since. This case was different. It would be rude to say "No," and this might be her last chance to experience something new. Besides, if she refused, Tippiny would call her ungracious, so she nodded approval. She wasn't going to drink too much, she'd just try it.

Mama reached for the six page menu, flipped through it, and studied the selections, amazed that some cost close to three figures. She noticed everything was a la carte and she knew what that meant. Many entrees were in French. She didn't know what chateaubriand was, but she dared not ask. That would show ignorance and embarrass Tippiny. When the sommelier returned with the Dom Perignon, he poured a small amount in Shannon's glass. She sipped it and nodded approval. He poured about half a glass for each person, and returned the chilled bottle to the silver ice bucket in the stand he'd placed by the table. Then, with a nod, he disappeared.

Taking a sip of the whitish liquid, Mama enjoyed the flavor. It was smooth. *It should be; it probably cost forty dollars a bottle.* She then took another and Tippiny touched her arm, whispering, "Drink it slowly, Mama." Then she slid Mama's menu aside. "I'll order for you. I know you like crawfish, so I bet you'll like lobster. I'm having that, too."

Shannon nodded in agreement."It's wonderful here. I'll have the same."

Looking at all the flatware didn't upset Mama. She'd read about how to use it--starting from the fork, knife, or spoon on the outside. The waiter returned and Shannon ordered an appetizer, escargot. Mama knew what they were. She wasn't sure how she could swallow a snail but to be polite, she'd have to make the effort.

What an afternoon this was turning out to be. She finished her glass of champagne. Shannon raised her hand for the waiter who hurried over to refill her glass.

When the escargot came, Mama was hesitant to try it, but she did and was surprised at its savory, buttery flavor. She ate two of them and washed them down with the bubbly. Summoning the waiter again, Shannon asked for another bottle. Mama wondered exactly what this young woman did in Washington, D. C. Did working as a lawyer pay this well? No wonder Tippiny wanted to get close to her. *She's spending money like it's going out of style.* With a few more sips of champagne, the thought left her.

She felt a little light-headed. *Dear God, don't let this be a vision coming on. I can't have one here.*

The food arrived on large, silver platters. The three waiters placed the plates on the table simultaneously, and then tied lobster bibs around each woman's neck. They also loosened the crustacean from its shell to make it easily accessible. Mama had never received such service. She enjoyed every minute of it. More champagne made her feel giddy and less concerned about watching everything she said. Goldie and El's granddaughter were sitting at this very table with her and she had an urge to talk. Wasn't this really the point of this trip? What questions would Shannon ask and when was she going to ask them? Maybe she was waiting for the right moment. *So, I guess I'll just enjoy this meal until she does.*

Only after they had finished the main course and ordered dessert did Shannon share her story. And she told the real story of her life, not the one she saved for the tea parties and professional gatherings of a D. C. lawyer.

Baked Alaska was placed in front of the three women and Mama hassled over which of the two spoons at her place to use. She finally chose the same one her daughter did, Then she listened as Shannon revealed some pertinent details about her life. By the time they sipped on an after-dinner cocktail of creme de menthe their hostess concluded her tale.

Shannon reached over and placed her hand on Mama's once more. Her blue eyes met Mama's and she held the gaze. "I remember my grandmother speaking of Cheche...you. She told me she knew you when you were a little girl. I was very young when she told me about that, but what I do remember is the name Tollar--I didn't call her grandmother, I called her Tollar--and she always called me Goldie. She liked to run her fingers through my hair. She said it reminded her of my grandfather."

"If she told me anything about her momma or daddy, I don't remember it. I was only five years-old when she died of a heart attack. My mother, Ellie, was in her late thirties when I was born. When she told my father she was pregnant, he said, 'Get rid of it.' She wanted me and he didn't, so he left. He was never a part of our lives. All I know is that I have his last name and I really don't want it. My father left and Tollar died the same year. Mom and I had nothing left in Mobile so we moved to Atlanta."

Shannon paused, taking a deep breath. Mama knew those memories were painful to recall. But Shannon pressed on. "I really knew nothing about my heritage when I was growing up. But when my mother died a month ago, also of a heart attack, I found an old trunk she stored in the attic. It had my grandmother's name on a label on the top, and was full of papers and an old record. When I started reading the papers, I found a marriage license for Eleanor Tollar and Goldie Parsons. And coming across the record was unexpected, too. Imagine how surprised I was when I saw Goldie's name on it! I just had to dig deeper into the box. I found a wedding photo, with their names on the back. Was I shocked! I knew then who he really was."

"I went straight to the mirror. I'd never thought I was anything but white. Had no reason to think otherwise. This was a revelation, unveiling a secret my mother wanted to keep. I held up the picture and I swear I could see my resemblance to my grandparents. Since the photo was black and white, I wasn't sure the color of Goldie's hair and eyes, but you seem to know, and I'm glad to find out. I didn't want to keep the secret any longer. I swelled with pride at being a descendant of the famous singer, no matter what color he was. I finally knew why Tollar called me Goldie. I did not know what to do when I got to this point."

Shannon squeezed Mama's hand. "Then your daughter came along. What a coincidence when I overheard Tippiny talking about Cleveland, Mississippi, and I remembered the letters to Eleanor in the trunk. They were postmarked in Memphis and sent to her in Cleveland, MS. I was so excited! I couldn't believe what I heard."

She finally stopped talking. Mama gave Shannon a comforting pat on her hand. "I can tell you lots, lots more, Child." She touched her forehead, rubbing the spot where the bullet had grazed her. *Now what do I want to say? I can't think straight.* "Oh, your grandmother stayed with us once when she came to Cleveland to look for Goldie." She removed her napkin from its silver ring and wiped her mouth with it. *When was that?* "Oh, er, I, I'm trying to think. Do you know the rumors? You don't know about Goldie going, er, missing, do you?"

"Just that Tippiny said there was an old Delta folktale about him coming back to Cleveland, and then he disappeared. What else is there?"

Mama's head fell forward and she jerked it back in place. "Excuse me. Let me think. Hmm--they never found him, until now, maybe. The bones they just found--they're his." She patted around the top of her dress for the stone, but it wasn't hanging around her neck. It was in her jacket. That jacket and the contents of its pockets were shoved into Tippiny's bag. It hung from the back of Tippiny's chair, out of reach.

Mama stood and pointed toward the door. "Tippiny, we've got to go. I need to get, to get, er, my jacket from your bag." She didn't explain why.

Not understanding her mother's behavior, Tippiny leaned over to Shannon and whispered, "Mama's not used to drinking. She's a little tipsy. Let's humor her." She summoned the waiter to bring her check.

Mama wasn't too drunk to sneak a look at the bill as the waiter slid the white slip towards Shannon who then laid her gold credit card on top. The total was enough to pay for a month's worth of groceries. Then she saw the amount of the tip and it appalled her. And she could have sworn the champagne price had an extra zero on the thirty dollars. When Shannon went to the Ladies' Room, Mama told Tippiny, "I think Shannon's being overcharged for that champagne. I saw where it said it cost three-hundred dollars. Shouldn't that be thirty dollars for each bottle? Should we tell her?"

"Good grief, no! Mama, it's Dom Perignon."

Mama's hands flew to her mouth. "Alright. I won't say a word." She couldn't believe anything to drink was worth that kind of money. It was too much to absorb. Fatigue overcame her. When Shannon returned and signed the receipt, Mama steadied herself with her stick and reached over to lean on Tippiny's arm. Tippiny got up and escorted her mother toward the door. Even with her help, it was difficult to walk, but she made it to the front of the restaurant where a driver brought Shannon's car from valet parking. Mama eased into the leather seat and put her head on the rest while Tippiny buckled her seat belt. She couldn't stay awake any longer. On the ride to the hotel, despite fighting it, she fell asleep, snoring away.

Mama Cheche woke up when they pulled up to another huge building. It was now dark outside and reality faded in and out. It felt like a vision, but she saw a porter in a red jacket and knew she would never have a vision about someone not significant in her life. That porter and Tippiny helped her to their hotel room. She heard her shoes click on the marble floor and knew it must be as beautiful as the floor in the restaurant, but she was too tired to take a look.

After assisting Mama inside the hotel and into one of the comfortable chairs in their room, Tippiny slipped the porter a fifty-dollar bill and asked him to order a pot of coffee. In no time he returned with the coffee and three cups. Shannon had slipped into the room at some point and was quietly sitting in the other chair. Mama drank about half a cup and when she looked up, she saw Shannon sitting opposite her. She still felt a bit queasy, but she didn't tell her daughter.

Shannon reached over and took Mama's hand in hers. "If you feel like it, Mrs. Brown, I'd love to hear about my grandmother and my famous grandfather." She seemed rather shy now, very different from the woman she seemed to be in the restaurant. Shannon looked down and smoothed the wrinkles in her linen skirt. "This is all so new to me. You will have to take my word for it, but I will bring you the proof that Eleanor and Goldie are my grandparents. I want to know their story. What do you know about them, their marriage, and his disappearance?"

"Honey, I knew you were theirs the moment I saw your face. I also knew because of the mojo. Your grandmother, Miss Eleanor, it all starts with her. Now she was one sweet young lady. No pretense about her. She was sincere. Her mama had her tied close to her apron

248

strings. But when she met Goldie and fell in love at first sight, things changed fast."

Mama shook her head. "Oh," she said, "I'm a little dizzy. But maybe I can get through this. It's important. Anyway, Eleanor's mamma was livid. She didn't want her daughter having anything to do with a black man. No, Sir. His being a blues singer made it worse. I knew it was going to come to a head, I have "the gift" and I *know things* before they happen, it's the mojo."

She got the words out before Tippiny could stop her, but her daughter's frown caused Mama to cut it off there and not mention mojo or the "knowin' of what was comin'." Instead, she continued her story. "One day, Eleanor told me later, Goldie had news that he got a chance to cut a record in Memphis and he came to tell Eleanor. That's all he'd planned to do. But when he got there, before it was over, Mrs. Tollar got into a tussle with Eleanor and Goldie had to intervene." She shook her finger. "That's when he whisked Eleanor away. Ended up they went to Memphis and got married."

"So they did get married? The marriage certificate is real, right? Wasn't it illegal for them to get married back then?" Shannon asked.

"Yes, in Mississippi, but they found a way around it. They went to Memphis. A couple of weeks later, Goldie came back to Cleveland, without Eleanor, to return Wylie Martin's car and he stayed with Wylie." She laughed aloud. "Mrs. Tollar told everyone Eleanor married a lawyer. Well, when Goldie didn't return for Eleanor in Memphis like he promised, she came back home looking for him." She closed her eyes and then opened them wide. "She reported him missing to the sheriff, but he was never found. She looked everywhere she could. Word got out that Eleanor married Goldie and things were rough here for her. Then she found out she was pregnant with your mother and she knew this was not a good place to be, so she left and went to Mobile. Some years later she came back, and stayed with me when Tippiny was a child. She was hoping to find her husband, but no such luck."

Tears smeared Shannon's makeup. She pulled out a tissue from the box in her lap and wiped them away. "That's so sad. Almost as sad as my mother keeping my heritage from me. But now, these bones turn up and it sure sounds like they're my grandfather's. Was he murdered?"

Mama took a deep breath. Her heart hurt from the pain of it all. She folded her hands and said a silent prayer. *How much should I tell?* Shannon is the one who can prove, or disprove, who those bones belong to, if they can get enough DNA. She took a deep breath, cutting her eyes toward her daughter and then on Shannon. Then she leaned back into the chair and closed her eyes.. "My head's not clear enough to discuss more tonight. And it's very late for me. I have to sleep on this."

It surprised her when Tippiny agreed. "Alright, Mama. Let's get you to bed. Shannon and I have a big day planned for tomorrow." Maybe she was afraid that the mojo would come up again. With this delay, she could warn her mama not to mention it. But would she comply? Maybe not. Mama could often be wilful. Tomorrow would tell.

***

When Mama Cheche awakened the next morning, her head was throbbing. She was rarely ill, so this was new to her. She eased out of bed, careful to not wake Tippiny in the other bed, and went into the bathroom. Everything was so fancy, even the bathroom, but her eyes were so bleary she barely saw her reflection in the mirror, much less anything else. She noticed the shelf full of complementary items: fancy soaps, shampoo, and lotion. *It all smells so nice and since they're free, I'll use some of these things.*

She washed her face enjoying the soap's rich lavender scent, brushed her teeth to remove the tastes from yesterday, and drank a glass of water. That didn't help; she needed a good cup of coffee to get her going. She went back into the bedroom and sat on the side of the bed watching Tippiny sleep. Should she wake her up? She looked down at her cell phone; seven a.m. flashed across the screen.

Feeling sick to her stomach and wondering how long she should wait for Tippiny to wake up, Mama wished she'd brought some kind of medication, but she hadn't. So she sought the next best thing--her mojo stone. It would be in her jacket hanging on the back of a chair across the room. Tippiny must have taken it out of her bag sometime last night.

Mama retrieved the stone from the mojo bag in her jacket pocket and rubbed the top. She didn't feel any better. She tried walking around the room and stopped at the window, noticing that the morning light was peaking in. Maybe Tippiny would get up if she opened the curtains. Drawing them back, she looked out and was surprised to have a full view of the Washington Monument. She gasped. It looked just like it did on her calendar. In the distance, she could see the White House. *My baby could be there one day.* The view took her breath away; for a moment, she forgot how bad she felt. But her stomach churned again, she really needed coffee, but she had to lay down.

The stone slipped from her hand and fell on the end table with a thud. Tippiny sat up. "Mama, are you all right?" she asked.

"I'm fine. I just bumped the table. Go back to sleep, Tippiny." Talking required effort, so she didn't say more.

"Okay, what time is it?"

"Seven o'clock."

Tippiny swung her legs over the edge of the bed. "I've got to get up. We're meeting Shannon for breakfast in the coffee shop downstairs at eight." She stumbled to the bathroom. "I'll take my shower first. I would've gotten a suite, but they were booked solid." She shut the door.

Mama didn't care. She didn't have the energy to take a shower, and when she'd turned it on earlier, water sprayed everywhere. She couldn't control it. So she'd just washed up. But she wouldn't tell Tippiny that.

Mama pressed her fingers against her temples, but she couldn't push out the pain. She picked up the stone and stared at it. *Mojo, do something. I've got to get moving. I can't give in to this.* She rubbed the top again mouthing the words, *I trust in the Father, the Son, and the Holy Spirit.* A flash of light filled the room. Her head spun as she saw images--a skull with a hole, a guitar in the hands of a man running away. And she heard the song *Reelin' Feelin'* as clearly as if it were being played on the radio. Then Goldie's smiling face stared right at her and he held up a record with his name on the label. *It's there! The proof is in the song.*

The diversion ended as abruptly as it began. Mama glanced toward the bathroom, afraid Tippiny might come out, but she could hear the shower still running. The images faded, rising one by one and disappearing out of the window. Mama couldn't stop her body from shaking for a couple of minutes. But when it did, her headache was gone and her stomach had settled down. *"The knowin' of what was comin'"* cured me. *Thank the Lord.* She gave credit to both the mojo and prayer, smiling at the thought. Now maybe she could enjoy her day in the big city. Like Mama remembered Tippiny did as a little girl, she got ready fast and looked beautiful in a matter of minutes.

Mama didn't take long to get dressed either. Her attire was simple. She got another plain outfit from her old suitcase, washed up a little more, and was ready to go.

Like dinner the night before, breakfast was also elegant and waiters stood by, available for every need. Mama had never had Eggs Benedict before and she found them very tasty. She was happy for the reprieve from her sick spell so she could enjoy them. Not only that, she was able to enjoy Tippiny and Shannon's company. With her last sip of coffee, though, she knew dealing with the real purpose of this visit--the history and the mystery of Goldie Parsons--would have to be faced. And soon.

After breakfast Shannon pulled up in her silver Toyota Camry Hybrid rental car and they slipped into the comfortable leather seats Mama remembered from the night before. Shannon drove around town, slowing down as Tippiny pointed out the sights. Mama had told them she didn't feel up to walking around, but she wanted to see the famous places. They passed the Washington Monument, the Lincoln Memorial, the Vietnam Wall, and were on their way to the Ford Theater when Shannon's phone rang. "Hello?"she asked, making it a question.

Mama and Tippiny knew something was wrong when Shannon pulled onto a side street and slammed her fist against the steering wheel. "Damn," she looked around. "Excuse me, Mrs. Brown, Tippiny, but this upsets me. They've got a crisis and I've got to go put out the fire. I'm supposed to be off today. I'll have to take you back to the hotel."

She turned to Tippiny. "You can keep the car and I'll get a cab."

Mama spoke up. "No need to do that. Actually, I'm tired and I'd like to take a rest. Is that alright with you, Tippiny?"

"Sure, Mama. We'll get some lunch and you can take a nap."

"Fine," Shannon replied. "I should be through about three, that'll give us plenty of time for Mama to tell me the rest of the story about my grandparents. I can't wait to connect all the dots."

When Shannon let them out at the hotel, Mama had her own dilemma. *Is it possible to connect all the dots? Will the mojo be there with me to do so?*

Chapter 25

After a lunch ordered from room service, an amazing sampling of fresh fruit and petite croissants filled with chicken salad, Tippiny offered to rent another car and do more sightseeing, but Mama declined.

"It's already one-thirty. We don't have much time. Let's just stay here and visit. I'm glad to have time alone with my daughter."

Tippiny agreed and curled up in the chair opposite her mother. They reminisced about old times when they shared the row house in Mississippi, Mama told stories of her mother Tippi, for whom Tippiny was named, and updated Tippiny about her childhood friends--who they married, their children, and what they were doing now. The conversation proved Tippiny was by far the most successful of the group.

In an effort to keep the mood pleasant, Mama avoided the two subjects that were taboo. Tippiny refused to listen to anything that had to do with the mojo, including Grandma Dee, and Mama shied away from the Goldie Parsons' case, saying she only wanted to discuss that when Shannon was around. *You won't like it, but the mojo's part of it and there's no way I'll leave that out.*

Mama yawned and Tippiny said, "You take a nap, Mama. I do need to check on some things at my office." She rolled the office chair over to the nearby table and opened her laptop. The sound of Tippiny typing lured Mama to sleep.

That was all Mama remembered until Tippiny's phone rang and awakened her. "Oh, I see. Well, it's five-thirty. Just come to my room. I can help you out with that." Tippiny hung up.

She looked at Mama as she ended the call. "That was Shannon. She is on her way here. She was scheduled to make a speech at a convention in town, but she can't make it. She wants me to fill in for her, apologize on her behalf and do a presentation. It's tomorrow morning at eleven." She sat on the bed with Mama. "Getting her confidence is a big break for me." She lowered her voice. "It means I can't spend time with you, though, and I can't leave you here alone. If I can get your reservations changed to an early flight in the morning, that's better than leaving you in a strange city to fend for yourself." She squeezed Mama's shoulder. "Oh, Mama, I'm so sorry."

Nope, no mojo there. Cheche could tell her daughter's words were sincere.

Mama smiled inwardly. She wasn't sorry. The few sights she'd seen satisfied her. She just hoped they'd have some simple meal tonight. She couldn't take such rich food for long. And she sure wasn't going to take another sip of spirits. *The only spirit I want in my life is the Holy Spirit. I think He's helping me now by giving Tippiny this opportunity. All I really want to do is go home. And Cleveland, here I come.*

"That's fine, Tippiny. You go right ahead. I saw some things I'd never have seen and that's enough. I'm old and I'm tired. I belong in Cleveland." She gave her daughter a peck on the cheek. "You have a life of your own; live it."

A tap on the door interrupted. Tippiny got up and opened the door to let Shannon in. Things weren't over yet. Cheche knew she wasn't off the hook. Before the day was over, she still had to tell her story.

After a few phone calls, Tippiny arranged for Mama to leave on a flight at 8:30 a.m. Deciding to order in again, along with ham sandwiches and potato chips, room service delivered a bottle of Pinot Noir wine. At Mama's insistence to decline, they only filled two glasses a couple of times until it was gone. Then came the moment of truth Mama dreaded.

"I know you need your rest for that early flight, Mrs. Brown," Shannon said, "so, before it gets too late, please tell me more of the story. Do you think those are Goldie's bones? What do you know about it all?"

Mama stood, leaned on her cane, and walked over to the window where she could see the Washington Monument again. "I was there," she announced. The two ladies took a deep breath and both were wide-eyed. "I was with Grandma Dee, my grandmother. I remember a shot was fired that grazed my head and then hit our porch ceiling. You remember that hole, Tippiny? Two other shots hit Goldie; one in his chest, the other in his head. He fell to the ground and the shooter picked up the guitar Goldie dropped and ran away into the woods. I was dazed but I saw Goldie somehow get up and run after him. Grandma Dee handed me a rag to put on my head, then followed behind Goldie, but she walked so slow. She couldn't catch up with them. It started raining something awful. I saw her struggling and went to help. My head hurt, but it was the mojo in force; otherwise, I..."

"Mama, were you really there? Don't let the mojo..."

"Don't interrupt, Tippiny," Mama insisted to her daughter. "I know what I saw and the mojo was part of it. My head cleared enough for me to remember it all."

"Okay, then. Who was the other man, the shooter?"

Mama shook her head. "I don't really know, I think I know but the mojo needs to show me more proof. Remember, we still don't know if those bones are Goldie's."

Tippiny folded and unfolded her hands. "This is frustrating. What can we do to prove anything?"

Shannon spoke up. "Maybe I can provide some with my DNA. Look, I don't mind being black. I want to know more about this part of my family." She grinned.

Mama unzipped her jacket pocket, took out her mojo bag, and held up a small notebook. "I may have additional proof in this book, too." She retrieved the mojo stone from the end table, and rubbed the top. "Whether you believe in this mojo stone or not, I do." She looked at Shannon. "I wish you had Goldie's record with you. There's something about it that is still to be uncovered, the truth is there, maybe the killer's name. But nobody, not even the sheriff, has been able to figure it out."

Shannon made a steeple with her index fingers and then touched her fingers to her lips. "Mrs. Brown," she said, "I don't believe in voodoo or black magic, but I can respect that you are telling the truth."

Before she could continue, Mama held up the palm of her hand. "No, no, Shannon. It's not either one of those two things. A bit of magic, maybe, but no voodoo, and mojo has to do with spirituality. Please try to understand that--we rely on the Father, the Son, and the Holy Spirit, not the devil." She put one hand on her hip. "You know, it's been said that Wylie Martin, a blues singer, tried to get Goldie to stop courting your grandmother Eleanor, and focus on his music, selling his soul to the devil for success, fame, and money. It happened at the Crossroads. Eleanor being white made Wylie more determined to convince Goldie to come down the path to perdition with him. But love won out and Goldie went with Eleanor." She shook his head. "Even to his death."

Shannon closed the gap between herself and Mama. "Did Wylie kill Goldie, Mrs. Brown?"

"Some say he did."

"What do you say?"

"I don't say anything. Not until there's positive proof." Mama clammed up. But she did ask a question. "What happened to the diamond, Shannon?"

Shannon looked at Cheche with her lips parted. "My mother had a diamond she said her mother left her. A family heirloom. Mother married young and didn't use it as was planned for her education. So she inherited it and sold it to pay for my college education." Her eyes narrowed. "How do you know about that?"

"I saw it once or twice." She didn't say it was in a vision; she let Shannon believe what she would. Then Mama clammed up again.

Tippiny knew her mother. That was all she was going to reveal tonight.

Shannon clasped her hands. "This settles it. I have to go to Cleveland. I will bring the important items from the trunk, and see this Sheriff Harley. I can't take off today, a Congressman got into a little hot water, and I have to put out the fire. But I can get things settled and be in Cleveland Friday." She turned to Tippiny. "You're coming with me. Please make reservations for me in your best hotel."

Mama heard a slight snicker from Tippiny and smiled. *Would that be the Shackem Up Inn? What in the world would Shannon think of those accommodations? No doubt, they'd be a surprise. So would other things, lots of other things. Miss Shannon was in for a shock, a big culture shock.*

***

Mama awakened in the middle of the night and sat up. She couldn't catch her breath. At the foot of her bed, an image of Shannon appeared. Her head was detached from her body and her pale face had a blank expression. Her wavy, red hair stood out, a perfect match to the color of Goldie's.

No words were spoken but Mama saw them in her mind's eye. "I don't know who I am. You have to help me." They came from the red-headed woman. Mama reached for the mojo stone still on the bedside table and rubbed it. It was ice cold. She took her phone and used the light to avoid waking Tippiny.

She opened the mojo bag resting beside the stone. Something prompted her to take out the notebook. She opened it, glanced at each entry, and turned the pages, squinting to read the small print. *Hmm, I never noticed that two pages were stuck together by that sticky red stain.* She eased them apart. When she saw an entry on the hidden page, all of the dots fell into place. Now she had more proof. But not quite enough.

She looked up as a record appeared turning and turning in the air. The label said it was Goldie's. She reached for it in the air, knowing it was a figment of her imagination, and it slipped away in a puffy cloud along with Shannon's head and body. Mama knew the answer was in the record, the one Shannon had, specifically. It contained the rest of the evidence she needed, the mojo showed her, and she could breathe again. Even though "the knowin' of what was comin'" made her aware that when the case was solved her time was up, peace consumed her. Putting down the stone and notebook, she pulled the covers over her head and fell sound asleep.

***

The morning trip to the airport went without incident. Tippiny turned Mama over to a porter with a cart and gave him twenty dollars to see that she made it on the plane safely. He did his job well and at nine a.m, the plane lifted off, on its way to Memphis.

The tall, lanky young man next to her offered his window seat. "Ma'am," he said with a Southern drawl, "would you like to sit by the window?"

"Oh, I don't want to take…"

"It's no big deal," he told her. "In my job, I fly a lot." He stood and they swapped seats. Then he held out his hand. "Gabby Brown, at yo' service."

Mama eased into the seat and pursed her lips. "What a coincidence. I'm Cheche Brown from Cleveland, Mississippi."

"Lots of Browns around. Ah, so you're from the home of the blues."

"How did you know that?"

"I'm a folk singer. Some of my friends are bluesmen, and women." He chuckled. "Can't leave out the ladies."

Mama's eyes lit up. "Did you ever hear of Goldie Parsons?" She looked at the blue-eyed man with no wrinkles on his face, and a head full of wavy, sandy hair. "No, you're too young to remember anyone from over half a century ago."

He touched her arm. "But I know the legend. Big scandal because he married a white girl. He disappeared in 1941 and he had one record that is still played. It is a fine example of how the blues merged with contemporary songs at the time. It made Goldie famous. Nobody ever heard from him again, did they?"

"Not until recently." She liked this young man and, needing to talk, she told Gabby all about the Goldie Parsons' Case in Cleveland. She even included the reason for her trip and some of the details about Shannon Edwards. She rattled on until after the stopover in Atlanta. *I need to get it off my chest. Who is this man going to tell anyhow? What I said to him won't go anywhere.*

But she soon discovered she was wrong. As they parted in the Memphis Airport at the Baggage Claim, he gave her his card. "You know, Mrs. Brown, I have a gig here in Memphis. While we talked, a tune and some lyrics floated around in my head. I'm gonna write a song about your story and play it before I leave here. Here is my business card. You contact me and I'll send you a YouTube of it." He snatched up his luggage and was gone before she could protest.

"Oh, my God! What have I done by blabbing all about Goldie and Shannon. That's not like me." All she could think of was the World War II warning slogan: *Loose lips sink ships.* She stared at the card. For the first time, she realized Gabby was a big time entertainer. He not only sang and played the guitar, he also painted and had become famous for both. Her knees weakened. She motioned to a porter and got on a cart. "My daughter arranged for a taxi to the Greyhound Bus Station." He knew where to go and took her where the cab awaited.

Mama didn't speak to anyone on the bus ride to Cleveland. She feigned sleep and didn't get off but once at an out of the way stop. She went to the restroom and then bought an RC Cola and a Moon Pie for lunch. A few hours later, when they arrived in Cleveland, she called Zita, whom she knew would drive her home. She wasn't sure she could walk and manage her bag.

"Mama! I am on my way! Don't move!" Zita exclaimed on the phone.

Mamma Cheche sat on a warm bench just outside the station and rubbed the stone in her mojo bag. Like magic, in a matter of minutes, she saw Zita's car driving her way. "Mama Cheche!" Zita exclaimed. "You're safe!" She leaned across and opened the passenger side door. "Hop in!"

Mama stood still, what was the big deal? "I can't interfere with your job..."

"Nonsense. We have looked everywhere for you! Where in the world have you been? We've been looking all over for you since that tornado hit. I'm sure happy to see you're safe and sound." She patted the seat. "Did you know your house was hit?"

Relieved to have a way home, Mama complied. "Thanks, you're a welcome sight. But I'm too tired to talk tonight." She clamped her lips together, being cautious to monitor every word that came out of her mouth. Soon enough, she'd be sitting in front of the sheriff with Shannon and Tippiny. Then she could blurt it all out. But not until then.

When they arrived at Mama Cheche's house, her chin dropped and her mouth hung open. "My porch," she exclaimed, "it's gone."

Zita drove around back and helped Mama up the steps that were still standing. She went in first and checked to find the house hadn't moved all the way off of its sills. She returned and told Mama, "It's all safe. Looks like just your porch was hit. I think we found what's left of it down the street."

On shaky knees, Mama surveyed the kitchen, bedrooms, and bath. The floors didn't give under her feet. She let out her breath. "I think the inside is okay. Thank God for little favors." She didn't say what she was thinking: *I can't afford any repairs. I guess I'll just have to do without a porch. Won't be for too long anyway. I can sure do without that hole that's plagued me all these years. Hmm, I slipped out of town without telling anybody to keep things under wraps about Goldie's granddaughter until I had more information. Wonder if that did any good. Only time will tell. But it's all bound to come out--sooner or later.*

Chapter 26

At two p.m. on Friday, Mama received a phone call from Tippiny. "I'm in Cleveland, Mama. I came with Shannon. We rented a car in Memphis. We haven't had lunch; we'll come pick you up and go to the diner. Can you be ready in fifteen minutes?"

By the time they arrived, the Delta Diner's lunch crowd had thinned out. When Levenia saw Tippiny enter she rushed over and stopped in front of her. "Well, aren't you something? Just let me look at you?" She sized her up and then gave her a big hug. "Mama tells me you're a big shot lawyer in Atlanta." She turned to Shannon. "And is this the Vice President of the United States you have with you? I wouldn't be surprised." She wiped her hand on her apron and held it out. "You'll have to excuse me. We're short-handed and I've been filling in in the kitchen. I'm Levenia, part owner of this joint, waitress, and chief cook and bottle washer."

Shaking Levenia's hand, Shannon replied, "I'm Shannon Edwards. You may have heard from Mrs. Brown that I may be related to Goldie Parsons."

269

"Oh--h, no. Word gets around fast in Cleveland, but I haven't heard that." She led them to a table. "What would you like to drink?"

They ordered coffee and surveyed the menu, ready to order when Levenia returned. All of them ordered the lunch special, meatloaf, with two sides--corn on the cob and sweet potato fries. Levenia returned with coleslaw and pulled up a chair. "This is complimentary." She looked at Cheche. "Have you heard the latest on the Parsons' Case?"

Cheche shook her head. "No, we're on our way to the sheriff's when we leave here."

Levenia nodded. "You're in for a shock. Zita just left and did she give me the skinny! Guess what? In digging through some old evidence boxes in the police station trying to find something new about Goldie's case, Hunter, er, Sheriff Harley, found a gun stashed in one of them. They also found a note and she gave me a copy to see if I can help figure it out."

She took a piece of paper out of her pocket and unfolded it, reading: *I'm hiding this in plain sight, ha, ha. I outwitted you dumbos. I bet you won't find it till I'm dead. When you do, IF you ever do, you'll be surprised to find out who it belonged to and how it was used. I've been to confession, but the priest can't tell you anything. My notebook might enlighten you, too, if you can find it. Maybe they'll clue you in to solve the mystery of Goldie Parsons. I wish I could see your face now.*

A waitress brought their order and they ate while Levenia talked. "It wasn't signed, but I think old Eli wrote it. He used to clean up the sheriff's offices years ago for pocket change. He also carried around a little notebook which he kept in his back pocket. He wrote down everything in it. I used to think he was making a list of enemies. "

Mama felt the mojo bag around her neck and the outline of the notebook told her it was safe. But she wouldn't reveal it now, she'd wait to tell the sheriff about it. Her curiosity soared, though. "Why did Rocconi give you a copy of that note, Levenia?"

"Oh, she knows I can dig things out of people and I like good puzzles. I reckon she's hoping more clues will surface." She tapped the table. "That's not all. They already found the gun belonged to Mr. Tollar before he died. They checked Mrs. Tollar's bank accounts and saw some hefty withdrawals about the time Goldie went missing. They just need to prove she gave the money to Eli." A group of six came into the restaurant. "Gotta go. Keep me posted.

They finished their meal and were served a complimentary dessert of banana pudding. "Mmm, this is the best I ever tasted," Shannon said as she savored her last bite. Then she paid the check and left a forty percent tip on the table. She smiled at seeing Mama's eyes widen and took her arm as they left the diner. "I was a waitress in high school; I know they make less than three dollars an hour. I can afford to tip big, so I do."

The sky had clouded over by the time they reached the sheriff's office. "I hope it won't rain tonight," Tippiny told Shannon. "Blues singers come to the Shackem Up Inn and people take chairs out and listen to them play outside. I want you to hear that. It's really good."

"I'd like to hear it. Oh, by the way, that record of Goldie's is in the trunk of the car. Should I bring it in now?"

"No, the sheriff doesn't have a record player. Let's wait to see where we can find to play it."

They entered the station and Hunter stepped from behind a counter with his hand stretched out to Shannon. "Glad to meet you, Miss Edwards."

He nodded to Cheche and then turned to Tippiny. "Nice to meet you, too, young lady. How are things in the world of lawyers?" He didn't wait for a reply. "Let's go into my office."

The trio followed him and found Zita waiting there, filing some papers. "We heard about the gun and the note from Levenia," Tippiny said. "That's a good break."

Mama pulled her mojo bag from its hiding place. "I have something else." She removed the notebook, opened it, and laid it on Hunter's desk. "I've had this for a long time, I got it when I cleaned Eli's house after he died. The writing's too small, so I never could read it without my glasses. I never noticed that two pages were stuck together, look at that red stain, until the other day." She tapped the pages with her finger. "Look at that. I could read some of it and it looks incriminating."

Hunter pulled the notebook close to read what was on the pages. When he finished, he slapped the notebook on his desk. "Hot damn! This is all we need. Old Eli just had to write everything down. This entry condemns him. Hell, he told all about killing Goldie and going to confession. Listen to this:

"Mrs. Tollar didn't pay me all she owed me for killing Goldie Parsons before she had that stroke. Ha, I bet they'll never discover the gun she gave me that I hid in the police station. They won't find my notebook, either. It's with me wherever I go. I'll burn it before I die. Nobody will ever know I killed old Goldie. Oh, was my Momma mad when she found out I'd committed murder. She said I'd go to Hell. But I won't because I went to confession. I told Fr. Jim Momma said to always do what Mrs. Tollar told me, so I did. That's what the fourth commandment says--*Honor thy father and thy mother*. He asked me if I knew the fifth commandment said *Thou shalt not kill*. I told him I had to choose and I thought it best to do what Momma said. I said the prayers he gave me for penance, but I didn't give back the money I was paid like Father Jim told me. Mrs. Tollar couldn't use it anyhow, she died.'"

Hunter's lower lip dropped. "Now that's as good as a signed confession. Ballistics proved the murder gun was the one we found in the station, the gun Eli said Mrs. Tollar gave him to commit the crime." He turned to Mama Cheche. "And you found bullets and a sales slip for them at Mrs. Tollar's; she was behind it all. We can also prove it's Eli's notebook and his handwriting." He bowed to Mama. "Thank you, Mama. Now tell us what else you need to report after all these years." He pointed to a chair and she sat in it. The others remained standing.

The moment of truth had arrived. Mama cast her eyes to the ceiling. In her bones she felt the full impact of "the gift." Now she had to call upon all of her energy and relive that horrible night in the Delta--standing in front of the row house with Grandma Dee, the trauma of the wild shot that hit the porch ceiling and grazed her head, the two shots that brought Goldie to his knees, seeing Eli retrieve Goldie's guitar and running away. Finally, she related how Grandma Dee released her hand, walked away and helped Goldie and they both disappeared into the Sunflower River. She sighed. It was all out now and it wouldn't matter if that singer Gabby wrote a song about it.

Mama made her excuses for keeping the secret. "I knew Eli would kill me if I told. He had a mean streak. After he died, since nobody ever knew Goldie was murdered, and Mrs. Elma Tollar was dead, too. There was nobody to punish for the crime, so why stir up a big scandal? Besides, it would only hurt Mrs. Eleanor if she found out her own mamma had her husband killed. Why punish the innocent?"

She turned to Shannon. "I hope this isn't too hard on you. You've had to adjust to lots of changes recently. At least you'll know your heritage, if DNA can prove you're Goldie's granddaughter." She sighed. "Some good will come of it."

"Sorry, but that's not going to happen. Those bones were in the water too many years for any DNA to last. We even tried checking the guitar; sometimes sweat causes a residue. Didn't work. However," Hunter stretched to his full height, "the gold tooth is Goldie's."

Shannon interrupted. "And I have the marriage license and a picture of my grandmother with Goldie, must be their wedding picture. Oh, I have the record, too. It's in the car. Where can we go to play it?"

Cheche clapped twice. "I know. At the Tollar plantation. Most of the furniture was sold, but a few pieces are still there, one is the old hand-cranked record player."

"Good thinking, Mama," Hunter said as he slapped on his cap. "Let's go."

Zita and Hunter took the patrol car and Mama, Tippiny, and Shannon followed in the rental car. Shannon got out first. "Oh, this old house is much larger than I thought. When I retire, maybe I'll pay the back taxes and buy it, keep it in the family." Although it was in disrepair and hadn't been occupied for more than half a century, Shannon commented on more possibilities as they wandered through the rooms. "I love to decorate and this house has charm. What potential it has."

When they found the record player in a corner of what was once the dining room, Shannon put the box she'd been carrying on the floor. Stooping, she removed the top and took out a very dusty record and handed it to Hunter. He put it on the player and cranked it up. As the vocals of *Reelin' Feelin'* echoed throughout the empty room, Shannon noticed a Manila envelope in the box. She hadn't seen it when she looked in the box before. Something was inside. Her hands shook as she slipped out another record with a label pasted on it with the names *Wylie Martin and Goldie Parsons.*"Sheriff," she called out. "What do you make of this?"

Hunter sized it up. "Well, I'll be damned! Looks like we found out why Wylie wanted Goldie to forget Eleanor. They must have had a deal going and Wylie didn't want Goldie to leave and renege on it. But he didn't kill Goldie. We know that now."

Goldie's record stopped on one spot and kept playing *E-E-Eventually.* Hunter checked it and found a scratch. He put the needle back in place and started it again. This time it stopped on *L_L_Levees.* Trying again, he moved it forward. That time it repeated *I_I_I got a feelin'.* Hunter slapped his forehead. "Good God in Heaven!

That's it: E - L - I. It spells Eli. Can you hear it? I'll be damned! The answer *is* in the song."

Mama let her head drop. The mojo was right. The answer was always in the song. What did this mean? It wasn't that simple. Goldie had written that song when he had no way of knowing Eli was going to kill him. This proved that he had "the gift"; he had "the knowin' of what was comin'." He just couldn't accept it, so he didn't use it to his advantage. Maybe the mojo could've saved him. But because he didn't rely on it, it didn't.

When the record finished playing the listeners all had tears in their eyes. Cheche spoke first expressing her thoughts about Goldie and the mojo. But she didn't explain that it often skipped a generation, nor did she go so far as to say it might be transferred to Shannon. If so, it would be her choice whether to use it or not. None of them argued with Mama, but they didn't agree, either.

Hunter tried to play the other record but it was bent, scratched, and cracked, so he couldn't get a tune out of it. So they packed up both records and went back to their cars. Hunter and Zita returned to the station and Shannon drove Tippiny and Mama back to the Shackem Up Inn. Before they reached it Mama said, "You go ahead and listen to the blues music, but I'm an old lady and this has been a long day for me. I'm tired. So, please, just take me home." They complied with her wishes.

Hunter took a bottle of whiskey from his bottom drawer. He didn't drink anymore, not since he couldn't solve that case in Texas. It had driven him to drink excessively, then he went cold turkey. Tonight, though, he needed to celebrate. The Goldie Parsons' Case would go down in history. He had redeemed himself. He poured half a water glass full and lifted it to his lips. Then he put it all back into the bottle. Except for being ignored by Jenny Stein, it had been reported in all the papers. Success was enough. It was its own reward.

As the sky darkened at the Shackem Up Inn, people brought out chairs to use while listening to the blues singers. It sprinkled, then stopped. So the music played. Tippiny and Shannon sat on the porch with a bottle of the best red wine Shannon could find in Cleveland and a couple of plastic glasses. A lady approached asking, "Shannon Edwards? I hear you're related to Goldie Parsons."

"How do you know who I am or who I may be related to? Who are you?" Shannon asked.

"Jenny Stein, I work for the Associated Press. I have excellent sources; I'm well-known as an investigative reporter and I'd like to interview you." She stuck out her hand which Shannon ignored.

"Sorry," Shannon replied. "I'm on vacation." She turned away.

"It won't take five minutes. I heard new evidence…"

"Look," Shannon stood and so did Tippiny, "please leave us alone."

Jenny raised her nose into the air. "Alright, if you feel that way. I'll just have to write the story as I see it." She turned and left.

"Sorry about that annoyance," Tippiny apologized.

Shannon waved it off. "Happens all the time. Forget it." She refilled her glass.

The blues men tuned up for another song and the lyrics of *Reelin' Feelin'* came on loud and clear but they had to stop on the verse with ELI because a downpour would have ruined their instruments. When thunder blasted out and lightning made multiple strikes nearby, all ran for shelter. Then Tippiny heard a clash of thunder and saw lightning strike a tree. "I need to go check on Mama," she told Shannon. They ran for the car as the rain came down in sheets.

Mary S. Palmer & Paula Lenor Webb

Chapter 27

Since Mama had no front steps, they drove around the back. The door was cracked open. "That's odd," Tippiny said. "Mama locks up at night and she wouldn't leave the door cracked even in the daytime." She rushed into the house just as the electricity went off. Using her cell phone's flashlight, she fumbled around while calling out, "Mama, it's Tippiny. Where are you?"

No answer. Shannon was on her heels. "I'll check the living room and you check the bedroom to the right," Tippiny told her friend.

Moments later they met again in the living room. "She's not here," Tippiny exclaimed. "Where in the world would she go in this storm?" A flash of lightning lit up the room and Tippiny spotted a piece of paper propped against the perculator on the counter. She snatched it off and saw the one page note was in her mama's handwriting. Her heart beat faster with each word she read aloud:

My Dearest Tippiny,

I have had a good life. Not perfect, but pleasant. I haven't been well this last year, but I was determined to survive until I knew what happened to Goldie Parsons. And not until I told all that I knew about the case. No need to repeat my excuses for not speaking up sooner. It's been resolved. I've redeemed myself now and I'm ready to meet my Maker.

Regardless of your beliefs, the mojo has been my mainstay. Having "the gift" was a blessing, and sometimes a curse, but it guided me through bad times and good. Grandma Dee taught me to use it wisely and I hope and pray that I did. It often skips a generation, as it did with you, and I have reason to believe it has passed from Goldie to his granddaughter. She will have to decide whether to reject it as her grandfather did, or accept it and let it work for her. I hope she realizes that Goldie had "the knowin' of what was comin'" when he wrote Reelin' Feelin' and he unconsciously left the clue about who his murderer was. It is worth consideration that Goldie died when the mojo probably could have saved his life.

I need the mojo bag with me until the end. You'll find it with the stone inside. It's for Shannon.

I love you very much and I hate to leave you, but you are more than capable of taking care of yourself. Go ahead and live your life. Godspeed.

Grandma Dee is calling me. I must go now. My Maker is holding out His arms.

Mama

Stuffing the note into her pocket, Tippiny let out a yelp as she dashed for the back door. "Oh, my God! Mama's going to kill herself, Shannon. Hurry. I hope we're not too late. Move over." She hopped in the driver's side of the car. "She's gone to the river. I know the way." She took off spinning the wheels of the car and heading down the dirt road.

After Shannon called the sheriff, both ladies remained silent on the short drive. In minutes, Tippiny pulled to the side of the road. "Here's where she'd be, I think. It's near where they found those bones." Hopping out of the car she flinched every time a bolt of lightning flashed. Now sopping wet, she walked down the riverbank aiming the flashlight she'd found in the rental car in all directions. Over and over, she called out, "Mama, come back. Don't do this. I need you. Please come back."

Phone in hand, Shannon said, "We may need more help."

Without turning around, Tippiny replied, "Just dial 911."

When her light hit an object on a tree, Tippiny stopped and jerked it loose. It was the mojo bag hanging on a low limb. She took it down and hung it on her shoulder. Then she said a prayer to the Father, the Son, and the Holy Spirit. Unable to discern the words, Shannon went to Tippiny's side and put her arm around her.

"We're too late. it's over." Tippiny patted the bag. "Mama's gone." She turned around. "Shannon, it's too late for me to bring Mama back, or maybe to believe in her, in the mojo." She took the bag from her shoulder and slipped it around Shannon's neck. "But it's not too late for you. Mama wrote in her note that she wanted you to have this. It's your inheritance. Take it in good faith."

Lightning lit up the sky. Goldie pointed to the raging river and screeched, "Oh, my God! A head is bobbing out there." She cupped her ear. "A voice--it's your mama. She said, "Shannon, remember the Father, the Son, and the Holy Spirit. The mojo is true, and now it's for you.'" The head went under and didn't surface again.

Sirens blared as a patrol car with flashing lights drove into the area. "It's a damn shame," Hunter said to Zita when they pulled to a stop. "We just solved one sixty year-old cold case of a missing person and up pops a new one, all leading to the same damn river. Looks like they're connected, too, in a roundabout way. It's deja vu, but from the report on the phone call, it's not another murder."

Hunter stepped out of the car rubbing the stubble on his chin. "Too bad that rain slowed us down and it took us fifteen minutes to get here." He pointed to two women in the distance with a flashlight who were headed toward them. "Uh, oh. Here comes Tippiny and Shannon walking slow. I knew we're too late to save Mama Cheche. Might not have been able to help anyhow."

Hunter shook his head. "Poor Mama; poor Tippiny. Hope we can find the body and Tippiny can get closure. Shouldn't take long to resolve this one." As he continued walking along beside Zita toward the river overflowing its banks to meet Tippiny and Shannon, he realized Shannon had gained something, too. She had found her roots. However, that last sentence about "not taking long to resolve this one" bounced around in his brain. He'd used those exact words about the Texas Case, a failure. Was this the mojo haunting him, or what? It seemed that the dirt of Cleveland had gotten into his boots and anchored him to the town. He lifted his chin and took huge steps forward, leaving Zita behind. *My problem. My job. Life must go on.*

About the Authors

Mary S. Palmer has a BA (Cum Laude) in English from the University of South Alabama. Her Master's Degree is also in English with a Concentration in Creative Writing. She teaches English at Faulkner University and is a member of the adjunct faculty at Huntingdon College. A native of Mobile, Alabama, she taught at Faulkner State Community College in Fairhope, Alabama many years.

She has published fifteen books, three plays, and numerous poems. *Boyington Oak: A Grave Injustice* was released in November 2019; *Tourism Writing – A New Literary Genre Unveiling the History, Mystery, and Economy of Places and Events*, was written with a grant from Faulkner University.

Palmer's short story *The Concrete Block Wall* won the Hackney Award in 2016. That story is featured in her book *Commas for Soul Searchers*. She loves to travel and uses those experiences in her writings.

Paula Lenor Webb, has a Master's in Library and Information Science from the University of Alabama. She is currently a tenured Librarian at the University of South Alabama, in Mobile. Ms. Webb has always enjoyed research and documented her local history findings in her first book, *Mobile Under Siege: Surviving the Union Blockade*, in 2016. She has continued pursuing this avenue of research with her latest book, *Such a Woman: The Life of Octavia Walton LeVert*. Mississippi Mjo... and Murder is her first fiction book.

www.ingramcontent.com/pod-product-compliance
Lightning Source LLC
Chambersburg PA
CBHW052026240626
47153CB00006B/1973